What Makes You Beautiful

What Makes You Beautiful

BRIDGET LIANG

JAMES LORIMER & COMPANY LTD., PUBLISHERS
TORONTO

James Lorimer & Company Ltd., Publishers acknowledges funding support from the Ontario Arts Council (OAC), an agency of the Government of Ontario. We acknowledge the support of the Canada Council for the Arts, which last year invested $153 million to bring the arts to Canadians throughout the country. This project has been made possible in part by the Government of Canada and with the support of Ontario Creates.

Cover design: Tyler Cleroux
Cover image: iStock

9781459414136
eBook also available 9781459414129

Cataloguing data available from Library and Archives Canada.

Published by:
James Lorimer &
Company Ltd., Publishers
117 Peter Street, Suite 304
Toronto, ON, Canada
M5V 0M3
www.lorimer.ca

Distributed in the US by:
Lerner Publisher Services
1251 Washington Ave. N.
Minneapolis, MN, USA
55401
www.lernerbooks.com

Printed and bound in Canada.
Manufactured by Friesens in Altona, MB in May 2020.
Job #265980

01 Let's Just Pretend

I GAZE AT MY FACE IN THE MIRROR. The eyeliner gives me raccoon eyes. My skills at putting on eyeshadow, rouge, and lipstick make me look like a sad clown. My shoulders are too wide and my nose too big. My dark brown hair screams "fifteen-year-old Justin Bieber." Why did I inherit this straight Chinese hair from my mom?

My *dàjiě* Dani, my big sister, wore this dress to prom a few months ago. She looked beautiful. But I just look like a boy in a dress. At my old school, a group of boys bullied me for being small and girly. What would they do if they saw me now? I'll just get beat up if I ever look this girly again. Maybe I'm just sick and confused. I don't know why I even wanted to try on Dani's dress and makeup in the first place.

I'll never look right. There must be something wrong with me. I don't know why I wanted to wear something pretty. It didn't work out and I'm never doing it again. I'm going to turn over a new leaf this year. I'm starting grade eleven in a new school tomorrow. I'm hoping that Rosedale will be more accepting. It's an arts school and I heard from other kids that people call it "the gay school."

"Loooogan! We're home!" The voice of my younger sister Wendy comes up the stairs. It is followed by the sounds of my littlest sister Sophie pestering Mom for cookies.

Oh no, they're going to catch me! I frantically look for my clothes. Somehow they've ended up scattered all over Dani's room. I'm still wearing her prom dress!

I squirm my way out of the lace and sequins and throw it into her closet. I don't have time for this! I manage to grab all my stuff and make it to the bathroom.

"I'm in the bathroom, I'll be right out!" I call out to my family. I'm pulling on my Captain America T-shirt and cargo shorts when I remember . . . makeup!

"Don't take too long like you men often do!" hollers Mom. "You need to help your sisters put away the groceries."

"Okay!" I holler back. I make a face in the mirror as I search through the cupboards. What can I use to take off the makeup? What did Dani use again? Soap and water? Girl stuff is complicated. I manage to clean off my face (mostly). I check to make sure that I don't look like I tried putting on my big sister's makeup. Like I hadn't just thrown on my clothes. Then I stumble my way downstairs.

"Took you long enough," Mom says. "I was about to ask Wendy to check that you weren't doing anything inappropriate in there." Then she turns to get a good look at me. Oh no. "Logan, you've got dark spots around your eyes. Have you been getting enough sleep?"

"I'm sorry," I say. "I'll try and remember to sleep more." I try to hide how relieved I am. My cover is still safe.

"You better! I didn't come to Canada to raise a failure for a son! And you're taking a big risk going to an arts school. Why can't you become a nice accountant or an engineer like your *dàjiě*? She received that $10,000 scholarship to study engineering at McMaster University!" Mom scolds me.

I cringe and look to my dad. He is sitting on the couch, pretending to listen to Sophie while reading a mystery novel. He isn't going to defend me.

I really want to say that my old school was killing me. But then Mom would only tell me to just *endure it, you're a man*. So instead, I say, "I got into a good school and received early acceptance."

"And if your grades slip, I'm pulling you from that school." Mom won't let it go. "You need to keep your math grades up so you can get into a good university!

As the only one carrying on the Osborne family name, you need to succeed and provide for your own children someday."

I resist the urge to roll my eyes or to run away to my room like Sophie does. I manage to say, "Yes, Mom."

Her dark eyes narrow to slits as she looks at me. That used to scare me when I was little. But I've learned how to hide my frustration from her, thanks to drama class. I agreed to take accounting just so she would let me switch schools. I figured out on my own I needed to change schools. I learned how to do it from a helpline for queer kids called Youth Line.

"You shouldn't worry so much about him," Dad says, pulling the attention away from me. "He's Chinese. He can survive whatever math tests are thrown his way. Or singing tests. He's a bright boy." I'm grateful. But he forgets that I barely passed Math last year. I had to get my exams signed and I don't like recalling how much they *both* yelled at me. And another thing I don't get — Dad is an English teacher and Mom is a secretary for a doctor. Neither of them are good at math. Yet they expect me to be? Dani is the only one who was ever good at the stuff.

"Hey, I need to practise for the choir audition," I say. "At this school there's even more competition for good choir parts. May I go to my room?" Maybe I can change the topic and show that I'm "responsible" at the same time.

They give me permission to leave. But I swear Mom is trying to find an excuse to keep me there . . . to do extra math homework or something.

02 Nobody Knows You

I ARRIVE AT ROSEDALE School for the Arts bright and early. From the moment I walk through the front door, it feels like I am where I am supposed to be. I spot a few kids with pink, blue, or purple hair. I even see two girls with undercuts holding hands. And a little part of me eases up a little.

When I arrive at the office, a skinny, white boy about my size (petite) with bright blue hair and a mermaid-meets-galaxy style smiles at me. He is holding a sign with my name on it.

My gaydar pings. I smile at him and tell him I'm Logan Osborne.

"Welcome to Rosedale, Logan Osborne. What pronouns do you prefer?" He gives me a quick once over.

I feel a little warm and happy from the attention. "Uh, I don't know about pronouns," I say. "And I'm, uh. Gay. That is."

"Welcome, Gay. I'm Robin Cox, your fabulously bisexual guide to the performing arts stream." He gives me a shameless grin.

"Boo. You're punny," I say, trying to hide the smile that I know Robin's going to see.

He cackles. "I was given your schedule by our sexy secretary, Mr. Talltree. I noticed one of your electives is Visual Art with Ms. Adams-Kushin. What you need to know is that she loves comics and she's also very gay."

"Yeah . . . I love singing. But I've been into comics and drawing since I was little. And, uh, it's nice to have a gay teacher?" I feel awkward as Robin walks me through the halls past a ton of other students.

"Well, Ms. Adams-Kushin will love you, then. We're heading to the music wing first for Voice class. Ms. Brown is . . . mostly harmless. She's the Filipino one. The other Ms. Brown is Ukrainian and teaches History. Stick with me and I'll help you ignore some of the haters in the class. You'll like my friends. We're all queer in some way."

While walking, I keep bracing myself whenever a guy passes by, expecting to be shoved or tripped. But it never happens. Robin keeps on chatting non-stop about the school and I nod. No one even says anything mean to either of us.

"So Rosedale seems pretty accepting," I say. "No one has tried to run me out of the school yet."

Robin stops and turns to me, his eyebrows creasing. Oh. I see he has really pale blue eyes. Nearly gray, but almost green, too. "Sorry you had to deal with that," Robin says, really seeming to mean it. "It's not perfect here. But there are enough queer students and teachers that the homophobes can't mess with us much. Would you like a hug?"

I feel my face flush a little and nod. Robin pulls me close and it feels good. I've never really been hugged by a boy before. It makes me feel a little more like I'm really gay and not making it up. But I'm still afraid to admit that I tried on my sister's dress and makeup.

Robin murmurs something and is the first to pull away. "You were really brave to just come out to me without knowing me. I barely know you. But I'm excited to be friends with you. And I know the rest of the group will be, too."

I step back from the hug. "I've . . . I haven't really had friends in years. Too effeminate and weird." I laugh awkwardly. "I haven't been hugged by a guy before. It was . . . nice."

"Well, you've made your first friend at Rosedale already. We'd better get to class before the warning bell goes off."

I nod at Robin and he nods back, grinning again. We make our way to Voice class.

With a flourish, Robin opens a door and proclaims in a dramatic voice, "We've arrived!" Then he turns to me and explains in a more normal tone, "Voice class doesn't really do grades. Most of the other arts classes don't, for that matter. I'm in grade twelve and my boyfriend is in grade ten."

I blink as Robin shepherds me into the classroom. It's different from the standard classroom in my old school. There are desks here, but at the far side of the room. The rest of the class is a big open space with a piano and music stands in one corner. And there are about thirty students standing or sitting around in clumps. They are chatting in what look like close-knit friend groups. Crap. I'm the New Kid and this is what I've dreaded most about it.

A short, curvy Asian woman walks into the room. She's in a conservative dress. The glint of gold around her neck turns out to be a cross. She wears her straight, black hair down past her shoulders and her eyes are a startlingly warm shade of brown. She smiles at Robin and me, still in the doorway, and motions for us to find somewhere to stand. We end up near where all the guys in the class are standing.

"Welcome back to Voice class, my treasures," she starts. "And welcome, new students. For those who don't know me, you can call me Ms. Brown. Choir begins next week. Everyone in the performing arts stream is automatically signed up as part of the program."

Ms. Brown starts right away. She gets everyone to sing, to get an idea of where everyone is in terms of vocal range.

Luckily, I have prepared for some kind of performance. But I didn't expect it so soon. After a few of the girls sing, I volunteer. I sing "A Thousand Years" by Christina Perri. I know it's cheesy. And *Twilight* is problematic. But the song hits me right in the feels. I really want to find someone who loves me like that. I notice a couple of the girls giving me looks — disgusted, unfriendly, or confused. If they were going to judge me for choosing a love song, I don't want to talk to them. I had enough judgment at my old school.

When I finish, Robin whistles and all the guys are cheering for me. A blond guy says, "Your high notes are amazing! I can't hit those. I'd love to hear you sing something by The Weeknd."

I feel my face flush again. I mumble that I can't do The Weeknd justice. But I can't help feeling a glimmer of hope that my time at Rosedale is off to a good start.

03 You Truly Understand

EACH OF THE GUYS sings for Ms. Brown. They are all awesome singers. And they are all really hot. What is this? A boy band audition?

Then this dark-skinned girl goes up. She has springy lavender hair pulled up into two balls like Sailor Moon. Her lipstick and nails match and she wears swoopy eyeliner. It's all put together with a leather jacket over a retro dotted dress. I can't pin down her background. Maybe mixed like me? We both have almond-shaped hazel eyes. But she looks badass! She looks around the classroom confidently and says she will sing "Know Your Name" by Mary Lambert.

It's the first time I ever hear a song that is so explicitly gay! I stare at the girl, amazed and a little envious of her confidence. And before I realize it, it's over. She is bowing to the applause and a few cheers from the rest of the class.

More than curious, I ask Robin about her. He tells me her name is Jennifer. All he knows about her is that he has seen her at a lot of queer youth events. And she sometimes hangs out with Kyle, one of Robin's friends he hasn't introduced to me yet.

Somehow, everyone has a chance to sing before the end of class. So Ms. Brown lets us chat with each other.

Robin flounces over to the guys and flings his arms around a taller, ganglier boy. "Micah! It's been an hour since you last held me. I missed you!" Micah effortlessly sweeps Robin up in his arms and pecks the blue-haired boy on the lips.

"Missed you too, bae," says the boy. "Even if you

make us out to be co-dependent to the new human." Micah looks at me over Robin's shoulder and gives me a dazzling smile. "Hey, new human. I'm Micah Deakin."

Now getting a proper look at Micah, I think, *Whoa!* His green eyes are really pretty. I've only just met these two guys, and I am already a little hot for them. Micah has luscious brown curls framing his face, and limbs like a giraffe.

"Uh. Hi," I say. My face feels warm and I'm struck by intense shyness.

A blond, blue-eyed boy pops out of nowhere with an open hand and an even brighter smile. I flinch. But I quickly recover and offer my hand to him in return. "Drew. Drew Dion," he says. "No, I'm not related to Celine Dion."

Drew has a slight accent, maybe French? It's pretty cute. I introduce myself back and another boy is introducing himself before I have a moment to gawk at Drew. My heart skips a beat. The first thing I notice is this boy's dark, puppy dog eyes and matching fauxhawk. The second thing I notice is his bared, toned biceps and black tank top. Why didn't I see him until just now? How could I have missed him? Oh yeah. New school jitters. And Robin keeping me distracted with his snarky comments.

"Hey, Logan," he says. "Welcome to Rosedale. I'm Kyle Hamada, the tenor section leader in choir."

"Jeez, Daddy," Robin pipes up from where he is wrapped in Micah's arms. "I know you can't help being a responsible goodie two-shoes. But maybe you could give Logan some space. Micah says he looks about ready to meltdown."

Kyle steps back, looking away and scratching the back of his neck. "Sorry, dude," he says. "I'm kind of new to being section leader. I promise to listen to what's on your mind and try to help out where I can. And if I don't, Robin's going to kick my ass."

"Thanks . . . I'll do my best," I manage to say without stuttering too much.

Robin looks like he is about to say something (likely a snarky movie reference) when the bell rings to end class.

I remember that I wanted to talk to the lavender-haired girl. I scan the room for her. Nothing. I dash out into the hallway, but she is already gone.

The rest of the day is pretty uneventful as school goes. Robin is a great guide and walks me to each of my classes before running off to his own. It's too bad I don't share any classes with any of the guys. I feel a little lonely without their antics . . . I also can't get Kyle's eyes out of my mind.

But by the time I get home, I'm not sure if I miss Robin's constant talking or if I want to muzzle him the next time we are together.

04 A Different Language

OUR HOUSE IS ITS USUAL chaotic place in the morning. How can it not be with three children (including myself) and two working parents starting their day? I wake up late and have to rush through my shower. I pick out the least muted colours from the wardrobe my mom bought for me. It's full of too much plaid and too many button-up shirts. I'm about to skip breakfast when I am called back by Mom while she's cleaning and helping Sophie pack her backpack.

"Where are you going? You have to eat. And you're not going to miss your bus today. Your father will be driving you to school, right, dear?"

Dad mumbles something in the affirmative and goes back to reading the news on his tablet.

So I have no choice but to sit down to breakfast. There's no bacon because Wendy ate it all. In fact, Wendy finishes eating first and leaves everything on the table. Yet she has the time to put on eyeliner and a pale lip gloss or whatever it's called before dashing out the door, yelling that she has basketball practice.

The drive to school is awkward. Dad is normally silent in the mornings, but today he wants to talk about something. "Your mother and I are worried about you," he says. "We know that you were being bullied at your old school. Maybe you should think about cutting your hair. Maybe wearing some of the clothes your mother bought you. Yes, I know it's embarrassing, but humour her a little, will you? She has your best interests at heart."

I nod wordlessly. My breakfast nearly comes back

up. I want to run away from everything my dad just said. I just . . . I can't handle it. But of course, I am trapped in a car with him. So I bring up comic books. "Have you checked out *Squirrel Girl* yet?" I ask. "It's the funniest series I've ever read."

He snorts. "Comics books have been going downhill for years. It's all the diversity hires. What kind of hero is Squirrel Girl?"

I sink into my seat and don't reply. Ever since I realized I am gay and am . . . effeminate? *Uke*? A submissive girly boy in gay anime? Yeah, no. That doesn't sound like me. I don't know what word to use to describe myself. But since then I've found it a lot harder to talk to my dad about anything.

We finally arrive at Rosedale. I hop out of the car and wish Dad a good day at work. But before he says anything, Dad frowns. He is looking at Robin and Micah holding hands as they wait for me. They wave. Robin is wearing rainbow leggings and sky-blue lipstick. Micah has on a bright pink shirt.

"Kids like you are ruining this great country!" my

dad barks out at my friends. Then he drives off without saying goodbye to me.

I look at Robin. I try not to burst into tears in front of these guys who want to be friends with me. "I'm sorry my dad is a homophobe," I choke out. "He said a lot of gross things in the car about a lot of people. I was trapped in there with him."

To my surprise, it's Micah who draws me into a hug. "I'm sorry," he says. "Robin and I are both lucky to have supportive families. You can always crash with one of us if the fam is too much to deal with. My parents are lawyers. My mom works for Justice for Children and Youth. She helps a lot of kids kicked out of their homes by homophobic parents. I know we just met, but you seem cool and you've got us."

I'm even more surprised that Robin joins the hug. He adds in a lower, more soothing voice than the one he used with me yesterday, "Micah's parents are loaded. If you need it, they'll come and pick up your stuff and you can crash with him until graduation. And you should talk to Drew about homophobic families.

I don't know all the details, but it might be good for you to have someone else who's had to deal with unsupportive parents."

For the first time in my life, I feel like someone gets it. Coming to this school was really the right decision for me. In that moment, I feel safe nestled between these two boys. I sigh and hug them back. "Thanks. I — I really needed that. I've never had friends like you two before." I feel my face heating up and can't meet their eyes. "So . . . you wanted to do stuff before school starts?"

The moment is over. All our arms untangle (except Micah has an arm still wrapped around Robin's waist).

"Just, you know," says Robin. "Hang out. No real plans. You're a baby queer. And maybe it's my mother hen tendencies, but I want to take you under my wing and help you take flight." Micah whispers something to Robin. Robin quickly amends, "Errr, mixed metaphors. But you get what I mean. You're a cute little twink like me in a culture that you'll find out loves to eat us up for dinner. And not in a good way."

I roll my eyes, feeling the awkward tension go away. "Do you want me to call you Mommy, then?"

Robin cackles. It turns a few heads. "Nah, it's all good! Can't be Mommy when Kyle is Daddy. Besides, wouldn't you rather be Mommy to Kyle's Daddy?"

I feel my face heat up. I'm pretty sure my eyes are as wide as a fish's judging by the amused expressions on Robin's and Micah's faces. "Uh . . . I don't know," I stutter. "He's . . . cute. Um. But I don't really know him?"

Robin cackles again. "We're kidding. Although, good to know." He winks and wiggles his eyebrows at me.

Micah jumps in. "We won't set you up with Kyle without your consent. No matter how much Robin here wants to Parent Trap you two." Micah pokes his boyfriend in the side, pulling a whine from Robin.

I feel lucky when the warning bell goes and we have to go to class. I'm pretty sure my face is lit up like a tomato, even through my slightly dark skin.

05 Between Us

IN VOICE CLASS, MS. BROWN says that today is a music theory day. Since we are a split-level class, with students from all grades from nine to twelve, we have different theory units to work on. She'll be doing mini-lectures with different grade levels and so everyone has to get into those groups. Micah is dragged over to the grade ten crowd by two giggling girls. Robin joins the grade twelve crowd. That leaves me with Drew and Kyle. And I spot Jennifer walking toward us, along with a few other girls.

Ms. Brown smiles warmly at me as she gets to our group. "I heard you just transferred here, Logan. I want to know what you've learned."

I meet her gaze and smile back, a little surprised by how approachable she is. I feel a little more confident talking about music. "They had music theory in my old school. So I know the basics for sure. We've done intervals, some ear training, scales, triads, major and minor keys . . . Um, that's all I can remember off the top of my head."

"Looks like you're doing pretty good," she says. "I'm going to leave you here with the other grade elevens. And I know you've heard this many times already, but welcome to Rosedale." Ms. Brown smiles again and hands me a bunch of worksheets to pass out to the others.

My eyes glaze over when I see what we are doing. Musical composition. It's like math. All I understand is that we are learning how to write harmonies that form the basis of choir music. Ms. Brown does a mini-lesson for the group of us and I share a look with Kyle. Even though I love singing, I've always hated choir. The sopranos are almost always given the melody and . . . I'm not a soprano. I can hit b5 and have the range to sing second soprano. But I'm never allowed to join the sopranos because I am . . . *male.* I'm not allowed to sing soprano. I hate having to always support the sopranos unless the song is written for *the guys.* And then I hate the words I have to sing. I hate being lumped in with the guys.

Voice class drags nearly as much as Math class. I don't think any of us really like doing music theory. But Jennifer at least looks like she is getting it.

The bell rings and I look up, searching for Jennifer again. I hastily grab my stuff and make a beeline for her lavender puff balls just as she reaches the door. "Uh, hey," I say awkwardly. "I really liked that song you did yesterday. I've never heard anything like it before." I feel my cheeks heat up for the millionth time in the two days since I started at Rosedale. Now that I am speaking to her, I feel small. Which is weird, because she is a couple inches shorter than I am.

Jennifer smiles brightly and looks me over. I feel like I'm being inspected. "Logan, right? Thanks. Mary Lambert is one of my favourite singers. She's fat, queer, and bipolar. I'm surprised you haven't heard of her."

"I just admitted to someone I was gay for the first time yesterday." I can't meet her eyes.

"Wait, you just came out yesterday? I didn't realize you were just a baby queer." I look up and see her palm covering her face. This is the second time someone has called me a baby queer. She takes a deep breath and straightens up. She offers me a hand. "I'm Jennifer Jin, local mixed-race, fat, crazy, queer girl."

I am confused by how she talks about herself. She sounds like she's on Tumblr. So I mention I am into comics and that my mom is Chinese. She squees and says so is her dad. Or at least mixed Chinese and white. Her mom is Afro-Guyanese. She asks me if I want to sit with her at lunch so we can talk queer community and comics. I tell her I need to check in with Robin.

I never expected to actually find another friend so

quickly. And, this time, on my own. Between comparing what comics we read and talking about what it was like growing up in our homes, I ask her about the girls in Voice class.

"They're a mixed bag. Half of the girls in the class aren't bad." She speaks between bites of the curry-like thing she is eating.

"Thanks for the heads up," I say. "Are there any other queer girls in class?"

"One of the brown girls is so deep in the closet that she's in Narnia. I know a couple bi girls and one demi girl. But I'm not friends with them. Tried to get to know them last year but we didn't click."

"What do you think about the guys?"

Jennifer shrugs. "They're guys. I see most of them at SOY. That's short for Supporting Our Youth. They run groups for queer and trans youth here in Toronto. I hang out with the guys sometimes if the straight girls aren't looking for a gay best friend. We're not close, but they're cool. I'm closest to Kyle. We sometimes swap comics and share stories about our families."

I sigh in relief. "Good. I'd hate if you really disliked them. I like hanging out with you and them."

"You don't have to worry about that. To be honest, I'd be happier to hang with them than with most of the girls in the class. If the girls are not low-key homophobic, they're low-key racist," she sighs.

06 Favourite Song

BY THE TIME THE FIRST week of school is over, I fall into a pattern. I hang out with Robin and Micah before school. Before Voice class, Jennifer chats with me about comics or gets me to listen to some queer band I've never heard of before. For the first time in my life, I have friends. Good friends. The kind of friends that don't make fun of me for being me.

It's after class and time for the first session of choir. I'm a little nervous. At my old school, I was singled out as the only boy in choir.

But Rosedale is different. We stand around in our sections (soprano, alto, tenor) behind stands placed in a half circle. Rosedale has enough money to have enough stands for everyone! And they aren't falling apart or rusty. I wave at the guys and they wave back with varying degrees of sass (Robin). I find a place to stand beside Jennifer where our sections meet. I notice unfamiliar faces, a bunch of sopranos from outside the performing arts stream.

As usual, Robin is curled up in Micah's arms. They look so sweet I feel like I'm going to get cavities. Kyle is talking to some girl I don't know. Drew is snacking on trail mix from a Bulk Barn bag.

Ms. Brown leaves her office and walks to the front of the room. "Hey! Attention. Welcome to the first choir practice of the year. I'd like to introduce you to our faaaabulously talented pianist, Drusilla Smith. Drusilla has agreed to accompany us. I'm really excited for the music that I've picked this year. Last year, you voted that we do all Canadian content and that's what

I've done. We're celebrating this wonderful country with the beautiful 'Requiem' by Eleanor Daley. We have a piece by an Eskimo singer, Susan Aglukark. And there's a Rankin Family song that features the guys' section! Yeah!"

I cringe as Ms. Brown points at us. About half the choir looks in our direction. I feel sick to my stomach and want to run away. I really like being friends with the guys. But being referred to as belonging in "the guys' section" feels wrong.

"Practices are every week," she goes on. "You're to know your parts by the end of the month. We have a midterm concert and then we'll be working on the Christmas concert. Second semester, we put on the school musical. We'll be holding auditions for that right before you leave for the Christmas holiday.

"I've given your section leaders instructions. You'll hear your part for the first time. The rest of the practice is devoted to section bonding. All right? Then break."

Kyle leads the guys — the *tenors* — to the next room where the keyboards are. The huge soprano and alto sections split up the main room where we have class. Ms. Brown is with the sopranos. An older Middle Eastern woman, who I assume is Drusilla, is working with the altos. Jennifer reaches out toward me in mock anguish as we go our separate ways. I stick my tongue out at her.

For once, Micah is the first to talk. He has a frown etched on his face. "Susan Aglukark isn't an Eskimo, she's Inuit. Eskimo is rude. A slur. And there are other holidays during December. A lot of us aren't Christian."

"I agree," Kyle says. "But we can bring it up with Ms. Brown later. For now, can we try out the part?" He shepherds us around a keyboard.

Drew takes a seat beside me. "We'll really need to belt to be heard over the sopranos and altos. But I would also like to have fun with the music."

I give him a small smile. He beams back warmly and adds, "I think Logan here would sound amazing singing a line over us."

I swear, my heart skips a beat. Drew has to be flirting with me. I see Robin and Micah exchange a look and Kyle's lips tighten. "Let's just learn the part for now," says Kyle. "We can play around with our part once we have it down. This is choir. We need to learn how to blend our voices together first. I get it, choir can be a pain. But we're developing skills."

Robin stage whispers, "Yeah. Skills in becoming sheeple."

That draws laughter, even from Kyle. "Yeah, you're right," Kyle sighs. "But can we just play along for now? We need to be strategic. Let's not waste the revolution on the first day of choir, yeah?" Kyle smirks and nudges Robin who, for once, is sitting in his own chair.

We all laugh and settle down as Kyle plunks out the notes on the keyboard for us to follow along with.

We run through the songs once. Micah, Robin, and surprisingly, Drew make funny faces, trying to break our concentration. This earns them a stern look from Kyle. After that, we play some get-to-know-you games. I find out that Kyle has two dads and a controlled seizure condition. Robin has a bunch of half sisters. Drew identifies as asexual homoromantic and Drusilla is his adopted mom. Micah has a rainbow bear that wears a leather harness and is named Bondage Bear. I don't believe him until he shows me a picture of the bear on his phone. It started as a gag gift from his big sister when he came out, and now Bondage Bear has his own Instagram account.

Choir is more fun than I thought it would be. As I go home and crash face-first into my bed, I realize I've never laughed so much in my life. I think about these guys who've welcomed me as a friend. I hug my pillow, feeling warm and happy. I've never had openly queer friends before. It makes me feel normal. I am a bit disappointed about more-than-friends, though. Drew won't be interested, given that I want to have sex someday and he doesn't. And I'm not sure about Kyle. He mentioned having gay dads. But is he into guys?

07 *The Stars Align*

IT'S SATURDAY AFTERNOON and I'm out in Chinatown. Mom did a grocery run earlier. For once, she didn't try to guilt me into doing homework, so I have some time on my own. I hit up the comic and anime stores first. Then I spend the rest of the afternoon wandering around the cheap stores along Spadina near Dundas.

I don't buy anything. But it's always fun to look at cheap, tacky souvenirs and pretty clothes and art from China. I end up at the McDonald's at Queen and Spadina to grab a bite to eat before catching a streetcar home. I'm looking for a table when someone raises their hand to catch my attention. I see a familiar spike of black hair and a sinewy frame wrapped in a Captain America T-shirt. Equal parts jock and nerd. He's so hot it's like I'm dying of thirst. And Kyle is a glass of cold water.

"Hey! I like your shirt," Kyle says with a grin. "Batman is pretty great. But Captain America is my favourite." He sounds more carefree than he does in class.

I feel my face flush and can't keep it from splitting into a wide smile. "Cap is great!" I don't want him to think I'm a DC snob. "I read Marvel Cinematic Universe fan fiction."

Kyle laughs. "Yeah, Jennifer told me you like comics."

I try not to sound too excited as I sit down with my tray of food. "Uh . . . Yeah. Grew up reading both Marvel and DC comics. I've been getting into Dark Horse and web comics over the past few years."

"Me too! My dad got me into manga when I was a little boy. It helped when I was in and out of hospitals. Then I found western comics on my own. Favourite superhero?" Kyle leans closer.

"It used to be Batman when I was a kid. Right now, I'd have to say Green Lantern. Specifically Alan Scott. He was my first openly gay superhero. Before Jennifer showed me more." I can't meet Kyle's eyes.

"Alan Scott is pretty great. Obviously, my fave is Captain America. But I'm getting into the reboot of Jem and the Holograms. Thanks to Jennifer." He chuckles to himself and looks off into the distance for a moment.

"Jennifer loaned me her copy of *Love and Rockets*. And I just bought the first collection of *Runaways*," I say.

"Jennifer is really invested in getting you caught up. You know, with the queer, disability, and people of colour comic canon. She didn't press as many comic books on me when we first became friends."

I remember to eat my fries. "My dad would disapprove of everything I'm reading. He's not fond of this push toward *diversity*."

"That's too bad. There still aren't enough people like us in comics. Or in books. Or media in general. More now than there were ten or twenty years ago."

I'm not sure what Kyle means by *people like us*, but I nod anyway. "Yeah. You'd think Dad would understand how important diversity is. After all, he married a Chinese woman and has four mixed-race kids."

"I'm lucky. My dad has always been really gung ho about exposing me to my culture. Too bad Japanese lessons didn't stick. My *otosan*, my birth father, works full time. So my dad raised me mostly when I was a kid."

"It's really cool that you've got two dads. It must make it a lot easier for you to be you." I hope that he'll mention he's gay, too.

"They're actually like any other parents. They're local queer royalty, so they can be a little controlling of my life. They especially try to control what I eat and make me stay fit. But I thank them for taking me every day of my life. My Japanese birth mother is pretty traditional. She didn't take kindly to her husband, my *otosan* coming out as gay and got sole custody of me and my *onesan*, my big sisters, when they divorced. But after I had my first seizure at the age of three, she didn't want anything to do with me anymore. *Otosan* and his husband, my dad, did want me and got custody of me. I don't see my two *onesan* much. They live with their mother." Kyle looks away. "Sorry for just blurting out my sad life story."

I feel my stomach drop. "That's fine! Totally. Uh, thank you for trusting me with your story. My life isn't nearly so bad. One *dàjiě*, or older sister, and two *mèimei*, younger sisters. My dad is pretty bigoted. But my parents are together."

Kyle smiles at me. "You're lucky. Broken families are pretty normal in the queer community."

I smile back. I'm trying to push down the butterflies in my belly. "Yeah, I guess so . . . We started talking about comics! And then all of our feelings. That got pretty deep pretty quickly."

"Yeah, it did. But I'm glad. I got to know you a

little better, Logan." He pauses and looks downward. "Uh, your fries are getting cold."

I notice he has a McFlurry. "Your ice cream is melting."

Kyle chuckles. "Guess we both got so caught up that we forgot to eat."

"Yeah. Quiet eating time for a couple minutes?" I suggest.

Kyle agrees and we eat our snacks in peace. In that time, I have a lot to process. Talking like this with Kyle makes me like him even more. I'm entering crush territory. But I still don't know if he actually likes guys or not.

My carton of fries is empty. "So I'm pretty new to the community," I say. "Where do I meet other queer people outside of our little group?"

Kyle is scraping the bottom of his McFlurry. "Depends on what you want. There are youth groups. There are online groups all over social media. And hook up apps, although we're too young to use them legally. There are some all-ages events, too. Buddies in

Bad Times is holding one in a few weeks."

"Cool. I'll check it all out." I'm trying to think of something smart to say. But nothing is coming out of my mouth.

Kyle breaks the short silence. "So in a battle between Wonder Woman and Captain Marvel, who do you think would win?"

"Neither. They'd team up and take down whoever pitted them against each other. Then Captain Marvel would ask out Wonder Woman," I say flatly.

Kyle laughs. I like making him laugh. We continue coming up with weird scenarios involving superheroes. It's nice. I haven't had fun like this in a long time. I've never felt it was okay to voice gay thoughts.

It's a couple hours before we part ways. We're both smiling like a couple of idiots. He waits with me at my stop until my streetcar comes.

While on the streetcar, I search for Kyle on Facebook. One of his photos has a rainbow wash. And there's a picture of him with two well-dressed men, one Japanese, one black. Those must be his dads. I frown. He hasn't put his sexual orientation anywhere. Nothing on his profile indicates if he is dating anyone. I sigh. It's hard to figure out if someone could be compatible when you're gay.

08 Break These Walls

MY CLASSES ARE GOING as well as I hoped. I don't care much for English, Math, or most of my required classes. Visual Art is fun and I'm learning how to draw better, but none of my new friends can draw. The class has a lot of guys. They all love anything Japanese. Their drawings of girls that are borderline hentai, or porn, make me uncomfortable. Don't get me wrong, I like anime. But I grew up hearing stories about the things Japanese soldiers did to Chinese children when they invaded China.

Ms. Adams-Kushin is pretty cool. When I first came out to her, she slipped me a link to *Assigned Male* by Sophie Labelle and said I might like the web comic. And when I came out to the class, a Korean girl came out back to me. She began sitting beside me in class. Her name is Jin-Seon and she idolizes Mariko Tamaki, a mixed-Japanese queer artist from here in Toronto. Sometimes, instead of drawing, Jin-Seon plays Overwatch. During free drawing time, she does little doodles of the worst guys in our class kissing each other and we giggle quietly.

In choir practice, after warm-ups, Ms. Brown tells us to pull out the song "Rise Again" by the Rankin Family. Even though it focuses on the tenor section, it really isn't my kind of music. But it's an easy enough song.

I really don't like the other two songs Ms. Brown has picked. I love singing. It makes me feel alive. But I can't get into singing the harmony line. It just sounds so . . . sad. I look at the sopranos and feel envious of them. I want to sing "O Siem" by Susan Aglukark even though Jennifer thinks the song is pretty boring. I don't care as much about "Requiem." But it still makes me feel unsettled by what I have to sing. And makes me want to sing what the sopranos are singing.

After choir, Jennifer leads me on the half-hour walk to the queer youth group called Alphabet Soup. It is hosted by SOY, and SOY is in the Sherbourne Health Centre. It sounds pretty confusing, but Jennifer assures me it gets easier once you've been going for a while.

On our way over, I tell her, "So the music we're doing in choir makes me feel uncomfortable. But I don't quite know what it is that makes me feel that way."

"Well," she says, "Minus Susan Aglukark, the songs are all composed by cisgender heterosexual white people."

"Yeah, I'd rather be singing Janelle Monáe or Beyoncé. Their songs at least mean something." I huff and try to catch up with her. She walks pretty quickly.

"True. And not that many of us in the alto section like choir either. It's all about supporting the sopranos. Ms. Brown likes to call them her *little angels*." She makes a sound of disgust. "What does that make us altos? The Sassy Black Friend to her White Leading

Lady?" Jennifer's lips are a glittery green today. With her mouth pulled in a sneer and with her hair down, I think she looks like a fierce Gorgon. Like Medusa, the snake-haired woman from Greek Mythology whose gaze turned people into stone.

"I feel weird about how music is composed," I say. "It's like you said. We're all here to support the sopranos. Being a tenor sucks. You altos get to sing the melody sometimes, but not us. Look at 'O Siem.' We tenors just sing 'oo' and 'aah' under all the girls. And I hate it!"

"I think it's because tenors are assumed to be guys. Guys are, like, not meant to show feelings or sound pretty," she observes.

"I love singing, but choir kills that love a bit. I always wanted to be a singer," I say softly.

"Don't give up on the dream!" Jennifer stops in the middle of the sidewalk on Sherbourne Street. "I want to be a gay rock star. So I'm taking classes in instrumental music. I'm not giving up. Music needs to be more fair and less gendered. If I can't find a way, I'm

WHAT MAKES YOU BEAUTIFUL

going to make a way!"

I stop as well and turn to face her. "Then I'll help you with your dream. You've been a good friend. I may not know what to say, but you're important to me. And it's not just because you're showing me the queer community. You're also the first Eurasian-*ish* person I've met who's like me."

Jennifer laughs and fans her hand in front of her face. "Ugh, I need to not cry right now. I don't want to ruin my eyeliner." She sniffles and blinks rapidly. "How about we keep moving down Sherbourne. We're getting weird looks from people."

So we keep on walking down the street and talking. "Speaking of Euransian-ish queer friends," says Jennifer. "I've caught you giving heart eyes to Kyle when you don't think he's looking. It's really cute."

I look away from her bashfully. "Yeah. I think I'm getting a crush on him. I just wish I knew if he is gay or not."

Jennifer squees and hops around in a little dance. "I knew it! I'm creating Team Kygan Hamborne.

You'd be so cute together! Asian solidarity! I'll try and get him to tell me in music composition class because I ship the two of you already."

I grin at her antics. It feels so normal talking about crushes. "So what about you? Meet any cute girls?"

Jennifer pouts at me and whines, "No. Most of the girls in choir are straight. Or they'd kiss a girl, but only for a guy. It's like a barren desert. And the ones who aren't straight . . . Well, let's just say they'd never look at all this . . ." she points to her belly ". . . and think 'I'd want to put a ring on that someday.' Especially the other Asian girls. Pretty sure I'm too dark-skinned for them."

I look her over and say, "If I was a girl and into girls, I'd be into you. Your sense of fashion is like, everything I've ever dreamed of. You could give Janelle Monáe a run for her money."

Jennifer leans in and asks if she can hug me. I stop walking and nod. She pulls me in close and I rest my head on her shoulder.

"You're really sweet to say that, Logan," Jennifer says.

"But not everyone is as awesome as you. The longer you hang with me, the more you'll see that the world can be pretty shitty. Especially when you're not just queer, but also fat, don't look white, and bring mental health baggage with you. Chances are, if someone is okay with one piece of me, they're not okay with another one."

I think about that and what it might mean for me. Even if Kyle is gay, am I too small and girly for him? I've never really dated before. But thinking back, no girls seemed interested in me at my old school. I think of all the clickbait about people not finding Asian men and black women sexy. Maybe it's true. I don't look like the Asian men that people find hot. I am small, effeminate, and nerdy. It's not like I want muscles. I'd rather be with a guy who is more masculine than me. What does it all mean?

But I have to make Jennifer see I understand. "If that's true," I say, "Then those girls really aren't worth being around you."

"I'm keeping you," she laughs.

09 When the Night Changes

WHEN WE ARRIVE at Sherbourne Health Centre Jennifer takes us to a set of elevators past a few security guards and up to the second floor. I don't know what to expect and am a little nervous. We end up in a room with a big table in the middle and a bunch of teens scattered around, hanging out. There are also a few adults.

Drew suddenly appears. He gives me a blinding smile. "Hey, friend. Never seen you here before. First time at Alphabet Soup?"

I turn to Jennifer, but she's joined three black girls a little way away. She turns to wave at me. I wave back, giving her a small frown and a questioning look. She mouths *later* and turns around again. That leaves me with Drew.

"Uh . . . yeah." I turn to answer him. "It's my first time at any queer youth group. What do we do here?"

"It's a drop in. We hang out. Get to know each other. Sometimes learn about queer issues or do some kind of activity. There's food and they give out transit tokens. The group is called Alphabet Soup instead of using the whole acronym for our community. It's easier to say than LGBTQQI2SA."

Drew motions me to follow him to the big table with the snacks and chairs around it. There's a short, compact, brown guy. He has a lot of piercings, tattoos, and a little goatee. He's dressed like he is in a punk band. He sees I'm new here, and introduces himself as Aidan, the facilitator of Alphabet Soup. I'm sure I look a little gobsmacked. Aidan is pretty hot. And I have never met any queer adults before.

As Aidan leaves us, Drew giggles. "You look thirsty, Logan." He pours a cup of water and places it in front of me.

I roll my eyes at him. "I know. *Toto, I don't think we're in Kansas anymore.* Give me a break. I'm still new."

The smug look doesn't leave Drew's face. "I didn't say anything. That was all on you, friend."

I pick a chip out of a bowl and throw it at Drew's face. He promptly catches it in his mouth. Chews. And swallows. "Thanks for the snack." He grins at me.

I can't help but grin back. "You're an asshole." I try to glare at him and fail miserably.

"Sometimes. But I'm just giving you a hard time. I think Aidan is hot, too. It's fine." Drew grabs a plate and piles chips, hummus, and cut vegetables onto it.

"I haven't met any queer adults before," I explain. "Or at least not ones I knew were queer." I look down and wrap a hand around the cup of water.

"Don't stress over it. I've been coming here for over a year. I was from out of town. So I was probably worse than you." This time, he pushes his plate over to me. The snacks on his plate are like a peace offering.

I give him a small, grateful smile as I take a baby carrot and dip it in the hummus. "Thanks. So why Toronto?"

"Montreal has a pretty strong queer scene, but I needed to get away from that city. Toronto seemed like a good choice."

I am pretty sure from the casual tone that Drew isn't telling the whole story. But we've just started really talking and I don't want to pry. "I've always lived here. I don't leave the city much." Then, changing topic, I say, "Robin told me that I should talk to you about family. Mine isn't . . . very supportive. And I'm not coming out to them any time soon."

Drew looks serious for a moment. Then I catch him putting on a seemingly easy smile. "My family wasn't great. I moved here on my own to get away from them on my sixteenth birthday. How are you dealing with your family?"

"I don't know. I try to do as they say so they don't suspect me. I once joked with Jennifer that I should bring her home as my fake girlfriend. But I don't want to do that." Wait, he was sixteen when he left home? And he treats it like it wasn't a big deal? I wish I had the courage to ask him more. I can't imagine what he's been through.

"It's good you feel that way. Robin's right. You can always talk to me if things get hard. I've been there. I used to hide in my room all the time and talk to people on Tumblr." He gestures giving me a side hug. I nod and I feel his arm wrap around my shoulders. It feels good to be touched.

"Oh! I do that room thing, too. I tell my parents that I'm doing homework. Which I am . . . somewhat. But then just stay in my room and read fan fiction."

Drew smiles at me. "I'm glad I met you. Here's to surviving homophobic parents. Want my number? I'd love to hang out sometime."

"Yeah, sure." I offer Drew my phone. Maybe he'll open up to me more later?

Of course, that's when Jennifer appears out of nowhere. "Look at you," she crows. "You're getting around already. Out for a few weeks and you're already getting a boy's number." She reaches into a conveniently placed bowl of condoms and throws a few at me. "Don't forget to be safe!"

I try to dodge the condoms, and I feel my face light up again. My connecting with Drew isn't like that . . . but she probably knows. I don't have a comeback to Jennifer's teasing, so I say, "I have to go to the bathroom, but I'll be right back." And I rush off.

When I get to the hallway, I see that both bathrooms are full. As I wait, who do I see come out of the bathroom . . . but Kyle!

"Uh, hi," I stutter. "Nice seeing you here. I didn't see you come in to the group."

Kyle seems surprised to see me, but quickly recovers. "Oh, I'm not here for Alphabet Soup. My *otosan* runs the LGBTQ Parenting Network down the hall."

"Oh," I say. How articulate! There's an awkward pause. We're just looking at each other.

"It was great bumping into you at McDonald's

the other day." Kyle finally breaks the silence. "You're pretty cool. I get why Jennifer became friends with you so quickly."

"Yeah, I had fun, too." Part of me wonders if Kyle is about to ask me out. How lucky would I be if I were asked out by a guy so soon after coming out? And such a hot guy! It'd be like living in fan fiction. Or the plot line to every gay rom com.

But reality shatters my thoughts when Kyle says, "I gotta help my dad set up the room for a presentation. But I'll see you at school tomorrow?"

As he heads toward a different part of the building, I realize I do need to use the bathroom now. I do my business and return to the Alphabet Soup room. I meet up with Drew and Jennifer and mention that I bumped into Kyle. We hang out and they introduce me to some other people they know. It's nice, but it's all anticlimactic after seeing Kyle. Before I know it, the group is over. I promise to text Drew later as I head to the subway with Jennifer.

10 Half a Man at Best

A FEW WEEKS AFTER my trip to SOY, I spot Kyle outside the choir room. I head over to say hi to him, only to see that he's talking with one of the sopranos. And they're holding hands.

I walk past as if I didn't see them and enter the classroom. Robin and Micah wave to me. I see Drew beaming at me. I wave at all of them and head straight for Jennifer.

"What happened?" she asks. She's on full support

mode right away. "Did one of the Chinese girls call you something bigoted?"

I look around to make sure no one else is listening. Then I say quietly, "I saw Kyle holding hands with some girl outside . . ."

Jennifer's Barbie-pink lips dip in a frown. "That happened yesterday. Her name is Stephanie Peterson. Soprano section. Oblivious to her privilege. Acts like a Disney princess. She's a Basic Becky." Jennifer makes a face.

"Thanks for giving me the heads up," I whisper to her.

Jennifer gives me a soft smile and pulls me into a loose hug. "I don't like her. Her friends picked on me in gym class in grade nine for being an out queer girl. Kyle can do so much better. You can do so much better. You're cute and a weirdo nerd. You're a catch and someone *will* notice it. Trust me, I know what you're feeling. Girls suck just as much as boys."

I sigh and close my eyes, relaxing into the hug. "Thanks for the pep talk. Boys do suck."

I feel the rumble of her chuckle. "No, you wish they did. And you listened to me rant last night about all my sad feelings and anxiety. You're good."

I thank her once more before Ms. Brown calls for choir to start. We take up our positions. We have only a few weeks before the midterm concert and we have to work hard to get it sounding perfect. I love singing with the guys, but it feels *wrong* each time I sing in choir. I cringe whenever Ms. Brown calls on the tenors. But I have to stick it out. Not only is choir part of my grade for Voice class, but I need to sing as much as I can.

When I get home, Mom puts me to work. She has done a grocery run, and the food needs to be put away.

I sigh and Wendy pokes me in the stomach. I yelp and stare at her smug face. "Hey. We've got work to do, dude," she says. She shoves the heaviest bag at me and I nearly fall over. "You're a guy, so it's your job to be strong and put away the rice."

I grit my teeth and try not to yell. I do retort while running for the sink, "But you're stronger. You play sports! And are actually athletic! Why are you picking on me?!" My arms burn as I lug the twenty-pound bag of rice and shove it under the sink. I glare at Wendy. "You're an asshole."

She guffaws and sticks her tongue out at me. "Hey, I'm not the one born with dangly bits. I'm just a weak, innocent girl who will faint if the wind blows the wrong way."

I see red. But I manage to rein it in by chewing on the inside of my cheek. I grab a bag of produce and begin throwing vegetables into the fridge.

Wendy keeps bothering me like every annoying sister ever. "Hey, I'm talking to you! Earth to Logan! Hey! Captain America sucks!"

"Wendy," Dad says from out of nowhere. "Stop pestering your brother and help me put the paper towels and toilet paper in the pantry." My shoulders sag in relief. I was seconds away from snapping.

"Thanks, Dad," I say as I grab another bag off

the counter. I've been avoiding him recently. It's been pretty easy since he's busy working on becoming vice principal at his school.

"No problem, son. We guys need to stick together sometimes." He helps me put away the last of the groceries in the right cupboards. Mom would kill us if we put them in the wrong place.

"How's school going, big man?" Dad asks casually.

"Okay. My friends are good. I think I'm doing well in classes. We're really busy preparing for the midterm concert. And then it's the winter concert and the musical next semester." I don't meet his eyes, pretending to scour the kitchen for any bags of groceries left to put away. I'm not going to tell him anything personal. It'd give him something to talk to me about. And I don't want him to ask me things I don't want to answer. Like about girlfriends.

"That's good," he says. I can tell he wants to say something. But in my gut, I know it would be something I don't want to hear.

"We done here?" I ask, looking him in the eye

calmly." I've got a lot of work to finish tonight."

Dad nods and I leave the kitchen. On the way out, I see Mom staring at a piece of paper with a frown on her face. Over her shoulder, I read, "Congratulations to Evan Johnson for completing his residency. We welcome him as the newest doctor on staff."

I remember that Mom once said she was a doctor in China before she met Dad. I'm sure that the new doctor doesn't have as much experience as my mom. Is this what racism looks like? I take another glance at my mom's face and slip away.

I make my way up to my attic room and jump on my bed, groaning. School is still pretty awkward. But coming home actually helps a little for once. Everything is still normal here. It's not awkward. At least, not the kind of awkward I don't know how to deal with.

I am just settling in when my phone dings with a text message.

Jennifer: OMG! I met a cute girl! :$ She's from our school, Korean, and definitely queer. We met in the girl's bathroom and she complimented my leather jacket and lipstick. And we got talking. She's a comic book nerd. I can't believe she's so awesome!!!

Logan: wait. is her name Jin-Seon?

Jennifer: Yes!!! How do you know her?

Logan: she's in my visual arts class. she's the only person I talk to there

Jennifer: OMFG!!! :$ I can't believe how small a world this is.

Logan: so you two been on a date yet?

Jennifer: Soon!!!! We're texting right now.

Jennifer and I go on to chat about everything and nothing. Her love life and comics. I am about to start on some homework when I get another ping on my phone. This time from Robin.

Robin: my anniversary with Micah is coming up soon. I was thinking of doing a flash mob and wanted all of you involved! Just dont know where to do it >.< ??

Logan: kyle said there was an all ages dance at buddies in bad times coming up?

Robin: omg thats perfect!! (>0_0>) im contacting Drew and Kyle now and see if theyre free. Ill keep you in the loop about meeting to practise the flash mob. I wanna do Lady Gagas Edge of Glory!!! =^.^=

Best Song Ever

WE GET TOGETHER AFTER school to practise the flash mob on the days that Micah has Greenpeace meetings and Kyle doesn't have swim practice. We meet at a park near where Robin lives just off Sherbourne Street. Robin mentions his mom is busy working as an emergency nurse at St. Mike's and so he usually takes care of his four sisters.

"How do you manage it?" Drew asks in awe. "School, choir, a boyfriend, and taking care of four girls?"

"By being a pro scheduler," Robin replies. "It's the only good thing I learned from the soul sucker, which is what I call the psychologist that tried to get rid of my autism. Micah helps. And I hide in my mom's room if she's not sleeping in it and let my oldest sister Felicia deal with the other three for a couple hours."

Practice feels a little weird without Micah. Robin is a little wilder and talks even more than usual. I can't keep up with everything he is saying. He gestures wildly at us, trying to explain how he wants a lot of jazz hands. Not even Drew can keep up, and he's the most extroverted of us after Robin.

Kyle nudges me. "Hey, Logan. Haven't chatted to you much recently. How're you holding up?"

"Pretty good right now," I say. "Even though I hate choir, I really like Voice class. Ms. Brown showed me how to relax the soft palate in my mouth enough to belt out the C above middle C."

Kyle splutters and shakes his head. "I can barely hit the G above middle C. You're really something, you know?"

I blush. I'm thankful when Robin frantically drags us into formation to do another run through of "Edge of Glory."

Before I know it, it's the day of the all-ages dance at Buddies in Bad Times. I tell my parents that I have a thing with the guys and that I'll be home by midnight. They seem pretty happy I am hanging out with a bunch of guys. I haven't had friends since puberty, when I began noticing boys and the bullying ramped up.

All of us, including Micah, are in Robin's room changing into club clothes. I'm wearing Hot Topic skinny jeans and a Lady Gaga T-shirt I've borrowed from Robin. As we change, the first thing I notice is that Kyle has serious abs. Robin starts cackling. "We're in the locker room, gays. Yassss homo. All the homo! All of it!"

Everyone laughs and I feel my face go red. Looking out of the corner of my eyes, I see that Kyle's cheeks are pinked, too. What? I look away and glare at Robin. As he takes off his shirt, I notice that he's wearing this black half undershirt-like thing. It looks really tight. Suddenly, all thoughts of Kyle blow out of my mind. "What's that you're wearing on your chest?" I ask.

Robin looks down at his chest and then back up at me. "It's called a binder. It's designed to keep your chest looking flat." He gives me a meaningful look.

Then it hits me. "Wow, I didn't realize that you were trans. That's cool." I try to play it casual. I think about how I would want someone to react and I don't want to be shitty.

Robin says firmly, "Yeah. I'm only going to say this once. I'm still a guy. I like wearing makeup and looking fabulous. And that means sometimes I wear my old clothes." As Micah gazes at him, looking love-struck, Robin gives the rest of us a hard look. "I'm still the same guy you always knew." He looks at me and smirks enigmatically. "And if you ever want to talk about how I knew I was a boy, just ask. I love being the centre of attention and helping caterpillars become beautiful butterflies." I'm confused. Why is he telling me about caterpillars and butterflies?

At last, we are ready to walk to Buddies. We are lucky it's warm for late October and can wear summer clothes for the dance. Robin and Micah show off their midriffs under neon crop tops. Drew is dressed like a raver in baggy pants and a black tank top with bright green highlights that bring out the blue of his eyes. Kyle has on a mesh shirt that shows off his biceps and abs. After seeing him, I can't take my eyes off him to see anything else.

"We should get moving, yeah?" Kyle says, interrupting my ogling. "We may be walking over, but I want to make sure we're on time."

I quickly look away. I know I'm likely blushing. Robin cackles but says nothing.

We line up outside the club, waiting for Robin's signal. Music suddenly starts playing from somewhere in the line of people. Robin begins singing the first line of "Edge of Glory."

Kyle pulls out a sign we conveniently left there.

It reads, "Happy Anniversary, Micah." Kyle, Drew, and I gather behind Robin, backing him up. I have zero dance skills, so it's a good thing none of us are dancing. But Robin takes up the whole impromptu stage, whirling around like a cyclone. Everyone in line (and the bouncer) has their eyes on Robin.

The song ends with Robin holding his arm out for Micah to take his hand. And as the last notes of the song fade away, Micah pulls himself against Robin. Micah's eyes are watery.

Robin is crying, too, but he's able to recover a lot faster. He holds Micah at arm's length and looks up at the taller boy. "You mean the world to me, Micah," Robin says. "Your gangly limbs, curly hair, and sexy rocker singing voice. How you translate human social interactions for me. How you accepted me as a weirdo boy without hesitation. You've been with me through thick and thin. I wouldn't be the man I'm becoming if it wasn't for you. You're mine as much as I'm yours."

Silent tears run down Micah's face. Now that Robin is done speaking, Micah pounces on him,

WHAT MAKES YOU BEAUTIFUL

bawling about how much he loves Robin and what an amazing boyfriend he is.

Drew starts cheering for them as they kiss. Everyone starts clapping and cheering for Micah and Robin. I feel like I'm watching fan fiction in real life. While I'm dying over how adorable they are, I feel a twinge of envy for what they have.

A familiar girl suddenly pops up beside Kyle. She kisses him on the cheek. "I filmed everything, *senpai*," Stephanie says. "I've already emailed it to Robin."

Kyle turns to all of us with an arm wrapped around the girl's hips. "Hey, folks," he says to us. "I want to introduce you all to my girlfriend, Stephanie."

I feel a little nauseous, but refuse to let anything show on my face. Robin and Micah are too busy being in love to notice anything. Good thing, because they would have noticed something was wrong right away. Stephanie is everything I'm not. She's a soprano, a soloist, pretty, white, and a lot less awkward than I am. She really is a Disney princess! She waves at us, smiling her perfect smile.

We all get back in line to get into the dance. While waiting, I text Jennifer, asking if she's coming. She responds pretty quickly, saying that she is actually on a date with Jin-Seon. But she says she'll be around later to check in if I need her to. I know I would feel better with her there. But I tell her to enjoy her date and that we can talk later.

12 Broke Inside

KYLE TELLS ME THAT Buddies is a theatre that does queer and trans shows, plays, musicals, and some community programming. His dads have been taking him to shows here since he was a little kid. In the lobby, I take down their info on my phone to look at later.

Once we are all stamped, we follow the thump of bass to a pretty big room. On the stage a short-haired brown woman is DJing and grooving to the music. It isn't packed, but there is definitely a good crowd going. It's a sea of Bieber haircuts, fantasy hair colours, fauxhawks, undercuts, feathery curls, and fancy 'dos that I don't know the name of. Robin and Micah prance to the dance floor hand-in-hand in their own little world. Kyle waves at me and disappears with Stephanie up the staircase in the middle of the dance floor to the balcony. I'm left with Drew.

Drew smiles at me. He offers his hand to dance. I shake my head. I really don't dance. Like, at all. He shrugs and disappears into the sea of bodies.

I make my way to the bar and order juice from the bartender. Then I turn around to study the crowd. I'm amazed to see so many people who look really queer. And there's more racial diversity than at Rosedale. I can hear Jennifer's voice in my head complaining about the lack of spicy food in the school cafeteria.

"What's so funny?" A voice breaks into my people watching. I turn toward it and see a guy that looks maybe a couple years older than I am. He's pretty cute. He has brown hair with the sides shaved in a very queer undercut and big brown eyes. His lip and one eyebrow are pierced, and he has multiple piercings along his ears.

"I was just thinking of something funny a friend said," I answer. "It's an inside joke, though." The guy catches me checking him out and steps closer into my personal space.

"You're cute," he says as he moves in close. "In an exotic way. Do you wanna dance?"

I back away by instinct. He is literally too close for comfort.

The bartender breaks in. "Hey, back up. Can't you see the kid is uncomfortable?" I turn to see her standing with two well-muscled arms crossed in front of her. Her fluffy, silver hair is shaved and shaped into a frohawk. I'm glad she's looking out for me.

The guy backs off, putting his hands up as a peace offering. "Sorry!" he says to the bartender. "I didn't mean to make him uncomfortable." Again, he holds out his hand to me. With that same confident smile he asks again. "Would you like to dance with me?"

I look at his hand and frown. "I don't dance, sorry.

But we can hang out?" I've never had a guy interested in me before. This is a good thing, right? This guy is hitting on me. That means I'm not ugly for being an effeminate Asian stereotype . . . right?

The guy retracts his hand and asks, "Do you want to go somewhere quieter?"

I nod to him and we make our way out of the room. Instantly, the air is cooler and just a little quieter. We find padded benches downstairs and sit next to each other. The guy, whose name I don't even know, sits pretty close to me. But he doesn't get as close as he was when the bartender told him off.

"Sorry again," he says. "I just thought you might be into me. You're really pretty. You're part Asian, right?"

I nod. "Yeah. My mom is Chinese. Um. You're cute, too."

The guy smiles widely. "Thanks. I love how smooth your skin is. Like porcelain. And your features are elfin. It's so alluring to me."

I smile back awkwardly. What he says is making me uncomfortable, but I can't say exactly why. Maybe it's the way he's saying it. "I like your eyes."

"Mmmm. Think you might be up for some fooling around?"

I'm about to answer that I don't really want to. Then Kyle comes stumbling out of one of the bathrooms with Stephanie hanging off him. I notice his fly is undone. Both of them have their hair all messy and they are giggling. They walk right past me and this guy, so wrapped up with each other they don't even see us. As they hurry up the stairs, I feel my heart breaking.

I know that they are together. And I know I'm silly for crushing on Kyle. But it still hurts to see it. My eyesight blurs a little and I quickly wipe my eyes with the bottom of my T-shirt. (Well, Robin's T-shirt.) I'm gay and don't have unlimited choice in who I can date. I'm lucky to be in Toronto where I can find places like this. But seeing Kyle with Stephanie reminds me how most of the world is straight and I . . . I'm not. It doesn't help that I'm still not sure if Kyle is bi or straight or what's going on there. On top of all that, I don't even look like the other gay boys around me. I'm not white. I'm not masculine or flamboyant. And I don't want to be.

The guy sitting beside me watches Kyle and Stephanie leave. "Looks like you know the guy," he observes. "Or the girl. And that you have a crush on them. Sucks to see your crush with someone else, yeah? You know, I could help you forget them." His voice drops into a huskier tone with the last few words.

I look at him and am reminded that I don't even know this guy's name. But I need something to make this hurt go away. At least this guy finds me sexy. He said so. Without even thinking about it, I lean over and catch the guy's lips in a rushed kiss. My first.

The guy exhales in surprise, but is soon kissing me. It feels like we are mashing our mouths together. I don't feel any fireworks or chills. Is this what it's supposed to be like? The guy presses me against the wall behind where we're sitting and I feel my hair caught under the hand that cups my face. I feel a little smothered pressed against the wall and into the seat below me. But it's better than feeling broken.

And then he's touching me. Between the legs.

I abruptly break the kiss. I push him away.

"C'mon!" the guy says. "Let me show you a good time. A little sucky sucky." He has a smirk on his face.

I feel sick to my stomach. This feels so wrong!

I shake my head, but he's on me again, touching me. "I want you on your knees for me. Isn't that what your kind wants? To serve a real man? A white man?"

I feel like I'm drowning. What happens next is a blur. One moment his mouth is on my neck trying to leave a hickey. The next he's hopping up and down clutching his shins. He's gritting his teeth and swearing in pain.

I kicked him in the shins just like I learned in self defense 101.

I get up from the seat and make a run for it.

13 Piece of Innocence Lost

I DON'T SEE ANY of my friends when I escape to the main floor. I try calling Jennifer, needing to talk. But my call goes straight to voicemail. I leave the dance without saying goodbye to anyone.

The trip home is mostly a blur. My parents are already in bed when I get there. I strip off all my clothes and throw them into my hamper the moment I get to my room.

I come back to myself in the shower. My skin is

red from the hot water and raw from the number of times I've washed it. I brush my teeth multiple times, trying to get the taste of the guy's mouth out of my own.

My face feels wet and I feel dirty. I wish that I could undo the past few hours of my life. I was stupid for failing to see the signs of a creep. I shudder when I recall the things he said. They made me feel like I'm a thing to be used because I'm Asian. And the way he touched me. I didn't like it at all. It wasn't just because it was him. Partly it was because it wasn't what I wanted, from anyone. I felt sick to my stomach when he reached between my legs. In all the fan fiction I read, the guys are into it.

Maybe I'm just broken. I'll just die alone with a bunch of cats.

I could really use a cuddle right now from one of my friends.

Morning comes and I feel more normal. I check my phone and see messages from all of the guys. They wonder where I disappeared to. And Jennifer apologizes that her phone battery died while she was on her date.

I respond to the guys, saying I'm alive but went home a little early. I feel like I'd ruin their amazing nights if I tell them what happened to me so I don't mention it. Then I ask Jennifer if we can talk about something that happened at the dance. She messages me back, saying we can talk when we get to school.

While taking the Bloor subway, I have time to think about what happened. The whole thing with that guy was pretty bad. I've never felt as dirty and ugly as I did last night. Yet for some reason, I'm not feeling that upset over being groped and hearing creepy racist things. At least, that's not all that I'm upset about.

When I arrive at Rosedale, I seek out Jennifer right away. As usual, she has her leather jacket on. Her lips are painted gold today. She offers me a hug and then pulls me into her arms. "Hey, so what went down at Buddies?"

Her tone of voice makes me think I must look fragile.

I frown. "I almost hooked up with a guy. It wasn't good."

"Oh, honey. Did he force himself on you?" Her forehead is creased with concern.

I explain as best I can what went on. From the ways everyone went out to dance to the guy coming on pretty strong. Kyle and Stephanie coming out of a bathroom. The kissing and the grope. And a little on how it made me feel.

When I'm done telling everything, I look at Jennifer. She seems pretty angry. "If I ever meet this guy," she says, "I'm cutting off his balls. He's scum. Racist scum. And everything he did was not okay! You deserve better. So much better!"

"I don't know about that . . ." I mumble. "Maybe I'm too weird to be dateable."

Jennifer doesn't look like she believes that. "Remember when I told you about all those girls not into me? I've been where you've been. From the moment I came out, all the cool, trendy queer girls didn't see me as sexy enough to date. No matter how fabulous I dress, they end up dating girls who look nothing like me. One of them asked me if I came out to get attention. She wanted to know why I hadn't kissed a girl yet. She didn't get that I don't have unlimited choices. I don't know how I met Jin-Seon, but I feel blessed."

It's my chance to change the topic and lighten the mood. "So could you tell me more about your date with Jin-Seon? You two sound really cute together. Cuter even than Robin and Micah. But don't tell them I said that."

It works. Jennifer tells me how she and Jin-Seon went to the Bata Shoe Museum. She gushes about how much of a weirdo nerd Jin-Seon is.

I'm really happy Jennifer has found someone awesome. But I'm still alone.

14 Ever Dreamed Of

THE MIDTERM PERFORMANCE is coming up soon. We're at the stage where we are fine-tuning our sound.

Toward the end of practice, Ms. Brown has some announcements. "Thank you all for all your hard work these past couple months. We sound so close to perfection. Keep up the good work. I know that we'll impress the school. And there may be a few talent seekers in the audience . . ." Her lips quirk up in a teasing smile.

"And don't forget," she goes on. "Auditions for the school musical are tomorrow. I'm really excited that we managed to score the rights to do *Phantom of the Opera*! And since we have a lot of LGBT people in this school, I'm encouraging everyone to transgress gender and sexuality! Try playing around with the gender and sexuality of the characters when you audition. It'll be fun! You're all very talented. I know that we're going to kill it! All right. Go home. Try not to put off thinking about auditioning. And as always, drink lots of water and keep those vocal cords lubricated!"

As people pack up to head home, I ask the guys and Jennifer what parts they are going to audition for. Robin grins and jumps right in. "I'm going to do a very gay Raoul. If Christine is a girl, he's going to be her gay best friend from childhood instead of her intended love interest. They're going to have a lavender marriage because he can't be openly gay. He gets a beard so he can find a boyfriend and Christine gets financial support and to live with her best friend."

"I'd kill to do a lady Phantom," Jennifer muses.

"Think about it! She's rejected as an outcast because of her scars *and* because she's a raging dyke. She falls for Christine's voice but doesn't know if Christine likes the ladies. Especially a lady with a scarred face. It'll be like the book version of *Wicked* — but actually gay."

I see Kyle talking to his girlfriend and feel a twinge. I want that. I want to be touched like that. I want a guy to look at me like that. It's really confusing, but I just want to feel . . . *pretty*. That's how I want to be loved.

I feel someone sling an arm around me and turn to see Drew's warm smile. "Hey, Logan, what part do you want to audition for? I thought it would be fun to be Madame Giry. She's not a very big part. But she's the one who keeps the secret of the Phantom. And I think I'd look cute as a strict ballet instructor."

I snuggle into Drew's side. I relish the physical contact. It's still a little weird for me, but everyone is becoming pretty touchy feely in this group. "Um, I really want to be Christine. It's actually one of my dream roles. And I could be a gay twink Christine with Raoul. Or a lesbian with the Phantom if Jennifer gets the part."

And then everyone is babbling in excitement. It's like fandom, with everyone talking about the feels, the character head canons of who they read as what identity and who's paired with whom. I look away from them all, a little embarrassed. When the clamour dies down, I ask Micah, "You're the last one here. What do you want to be?"

Micah shrugs and slings his pansy-printed backpack over his shoulder. "I'm good with whatever. Maybe Meg Giry? I know I look good in ballet tights. I still have a musical to be in two years from now. This is for the rest of you. It's your time to shine."

"Awww, but I want you to have fun, too," Robin says. "Maybe we could be Carlotta and Piangi so we can sing together. I can see us as stuck-up opera singers together. Although I'm not sure which I'd like better. Being sassy and loud, or getting to die a gruesome death on stage."

Robin's gaze falls on Kyle and Stephanie and

his lips curve into a sardonic smile. He is planning something. And I know I won't like it.

I shoot him a glare and he flips me the bird. "Hey," he says. "Maybe if we can drag Kyle away from Stephanie, we can hang out at Micah's place. His parents have a sweet entertainment room for Netflix and platonic chilling."

"Can I bring the girl I'm dating?" Jennifer asks. "Even if you're all pretty gay, there's too much testosterone in this group." She rolls her eyes. I'm a bit surprised she wants to join in with the guys. But she's been hanging out with all of us recently.

"Sure, the more, the merrier," says Micah. "Just let me text my parents."

And once again, I'm struck by how normal and good this feels. I have friends. And awkward crush feelings. I feel the memories from the dance party move to the back of my mind as I watch Drew join Micah and Robin in a game of grab-ass and hear Jennifer sighing about the behaviour of *boys*.

15 *Sounds Like You*

MOM BOUGHT ME THIS SUIT. I hate how it emphasizes my shoulders. She insists that it makes me look handsome and I just feel like throwing up. I hate putting on a tie. I hate how the white dress shirt looks on me. And the suit jacket feels too baggy and looks dull when I want to shine.

During the dress rehearsal right before the mid-term concert, I look to the girls (including Jennifer) and wish I could be wearing something red like they are. I tell this to Jennifer and she makes a sympathetic noise. "Yeah, wearing cute dresses can be pretty great if you like them. Gender norms suck. Maybe I can take you shopping some time. We can have fun trying on whatever clothes we find at Value Village."

I agree with her and we make plans to do that. Butterflies flutter in my belly and I don't quite get it. But I'm excited at the thought of buying clothes I want instead of what my mom buys for me.

During dinner break before going on stage, I catch a flash of red on Micah's hands. Robin is painting Micah's nails. Robin grins at me and Micah waves me over.

"I could never get away with painting my nails like that," I tell them. "My mom would probably ship me off to stay with her sister in China. And my dad would disown me."

"There. Now we wait for them to dry a bit, then we can put on a top coat," says Robin. "Logan, let me do your nails. I was going to do everyone's so we can all match. We can get rid of it after the performance. It'll be fun."

"Uh . . . Okay?" I'm not sure why I agree to it. But when it's done, I stare at my nails. The little bits of red glitter catch the light. It's really pretty.

"Red is a good colour on you," says Robin. "You know, the way you're staring at your nails right now reminds me of the first time I put on a binder. I didn't know what I was missing. Then I saw what I looked like with a flat chest. And I started crying. I didn't even know I was trans until then. I had been told by my creepy child psychologist that my gender was just a special interest. That it wasn't real."

I give Robin a confused look. So he explains, "I still liked pretty things and makeup. I was also autistic. They didn't believe I was a boy because of all that. They didn't realize I could be a boy. A really fabulous boy who sometimes likes wearing makeup and dresses. It's not a fixation on gender."

Micah's been listening this whole while. He adds casually, "What he's trying to say is that your nails look really cute. And that you look happier with your nails painted than we've seen you in a long time."

"Oh . . ." is all I can say. Part of me wants to be angry at the two of them to even hint that I am trans. But then I realize that's not what they said. Maybe I'm like Robin. Maybe I'm a boy who likes having my nails painted and fabulous clothes. Maybe he'd let me try on some of his clothes? I know for sure I don't want to be the same as the boys around me. But it's what I want to be that I'm not sure of.

Robin watches me process this. "Let me know if you ever want to talk or need help with something. I know I talk too much and I'm annoying. But I also know a little about being bullied." Robin sounds so serious he seems older than I'm used to seeing him.

"Thanks for everything that you two have done for me," I say finally. "Would it be too much for you to stand with me during the performance? Today has been pretty bad."

Robin motions for a hug. I let him and Micah wrap me up in their arms again. I feel really safe between them.

The other guys have their nails done and we stand

as a group. Micah and Robin flank me during the performance. Drew shoots me a worried look so I nod and give him a small smile. Kyle nods and I think I see something bordering on affection in his eyes. And Jennifer gives me a thumbs up. My phone buzzes. It's a text from Jennifer that she approves of my self care.

The week after the midterm concert, Ms. Brown breaks out the music for the holiday concert. As she passes the sheet music to the section leaders, she excitedly says it is her favourite time of year and gushes over the songs.

Kyle hands out the sheet music to all of us. I flip through the booklets. It's all typical fare. "Santa Baby," "Little Drummer Boy," "We Three Kings," and "Baby, It's Cold Outside." Ms. Brown tells us there will be soloists for every song and a duet for "Baby, It's Cold Outside."

I spot Micah scowling, his forehead creased in a way I've never seen before. Our usually easy-going hippy looks pretty upset. He interrupts Ms. Brown to say, "Why is it that all these songs either are Christian or degrade women?"

Ms. Brown's smile fades and she places her hands on her hips. "I'm sorry, but Christmas is part of this holiday season. *Glee* did a cover of 'Baby, It's Cold Outside' with two guys. It was a gay romance number. I'm sorry. I thought about the LGBT community when I picked these songs."

Micah retorts with controlled anger. "You call this a holiday concert, but it's clearly not. Not everyone is Christian. There are many other holidays around this time. Just in choir there are ten of us who are Jewish."

One of the girls from the soprano section pipes up. "I'm Jewish and I don't mind Christmas songs. Micah, why are you making such a big of deal of it?"

Jennifer jumps in. "Because it's really shitty when the system says that you don't matter!" She glares at the soprano.

"Oh, oh, I'm triggered!" says a girl in a mocking voice.

At that, the whole choir erupts. Most of the girls are yelling at Jennifer and Micah.

Robin promptly steps out in front of Micah, shielding him and giving the girls a withering glare. Kyle does the same thing for Jennifer. I quickly step up to shield her, too, as Drew joins Robin in protecting Micah.

I feel Jennifer clutch me, shivering in my arms. I focus on holding her, and let Kyle take on the role of being a human wall.

It happens so quickly, but ends just as suddenly. The lights are turned on and off and the clash of a cymbal stops the yelling. I turn to see Drew's mom Drusilla with one hand on the light switch and a drumstick in the other. Normally, Drusilla looks like any middle-aged Middle Eastern woman on the street. But seeing her standing there, I realize I never noticed how tall she actually is. Seeing her with her eyes narrowed, I'm glad she isn't glaring at me.

Ms. Brown is curled up in the corner, crying. I feel a little sorry for her, but more grateful that Drusilla stepped up. The room is dead silent except for Ms. Brown's soft sobbing. Then Drusilla finally speaks. Her voice is soft, but I'm sure everyone hears it. "That's enough of that. Girls, you should be ashamed of yourselves. You may not agree, but that doesn't mean you are allowed to bully someone. Don't make me do this again or I'm getting the vice principal involved. Ms. Brown had one last announcement for today. The casting for *Phantom* is posted outside the auditorium. Choir dismissed."

16 Must Be Fireproof

EVERYONE GETS READY TO LEAVE. I spot Drusilla checking up on Ms. Brown so I direct my attention back to Jennifer. Her face is buried in Kyle's neck and she is clutching his shirt like it's a lifeline. I quickly glance over to see Robin comforting Micah. He is speaking to him in a low voice while Drew makes his way to his mom.

I recall what Jennifer told me in case she ever has a breakdown. I ask her, "Do you want to move somewhere out of the room? Maybe the bathroom?"

Kyle looks thankful for my question. When I hear a muffled "uh huh" from Kyle's neck, I grab all our stuff. Kyle and I each offer Jennifer an arm. She agrees again and we flank her as she makes her way to the bathroom.

I frown as we near the two gendered bathrooms. It's times like this I wish bathrooms weren't so gendered. Luckily, no one is there. We enter the girls' bathroom and Kyle locks the door behind us.

"Hey, do you want something to eat or drink right now?" Kyle's voice is pitched softer than I've ever heard it.

"N-no," replies Jennifer. "Just grab my makeup remover and the wipes. Thanks. Both of you." Jennifer grabs a paper towel and blows her nose into it.

"Anytime," Kyle says. "You're my lesbro. I just wish I could have done more to protect you." He motions that he wants to rub her shoulders and Jennifer nods.

I find Jennifer's makeup stuff and bring it over to the sink.

Jennifer looks at herself in the mirror. "Ugh, my makeup is all messed up. My femme armour broke. And I love you, Kyle. You, too, Logan. I'm feeling mostly okay thanks to both of you coming to my rescue. Do you think Ms. Brown will let me defect from the altos and come sing with you guys? I can sing high tenor." She starts washing her makeup off.

It's weird seeing Jennifer without anything on her face. Her eyes look smaller without winged tips making them cat eyes. I miss her rainbow of lipsticks.

"I think so," says Kyle. "There's a lot of altos already and we're a pretty small section. Anything else you need right now? The girls were pretty nasty." Kyle glances at me to see if I know anything else we should be doing to help our friend.

"Once I'm done this, let's gather up the guys if they're still there," says Jennifer. "We'll check out the casting. I just want to get this over with. And I really need boba and dumplings for self care afterward. Think you can both come with?"

Kyle and I chime in at the same time, agreeing

to bubble tea and dumplings later. As I look at Kyle, blushing, I spot a small smile gracing the corner of Jennifer's lips.

"All right, I'm done. Let's get out of here and find out our sentence for the next few months." Jennifer points toward the door and strides out like a warrior to battle. Which I guess she is. I don't think I could have recovered from being yelled at like that so quickly.

Micah and Robin are still in the classroom and we hail them over. I see Drew talking quietly with Drusilla. I'm thankful that there is no sign of Ms. Brown.

Drusilla says to the group, "Good luck. And if any of you need to talk about what happened today, ask Drew. We can schedule a time to meet. I've got to report the incident to the office and fill out the paperwork since Ms. Brown left." She rolls her eyes and makes a face like she ate something sour. She walks with us out the door and leaves us at the auditorium.

No one else is there so we don't have to fight to see the results. Each of my friends goes up to search the list for their name.

"That lying, racist, transphobic, homophobic piece of shit! She cast me as the Phantom! I don't mind being the leading man, but I don't want to kiss Stephanie!" Robin shrieks and balls his fists. "No offence, Kyle," he adds.

And that means that Stephanie is Christine. I feel pretty bummed about not getting the part. It stings extra hard because it's Stephanie, the girl who gets to date Kyle, that gets the part I wanted. I fight down the feelings of jealousy.

Micah is next. He groans and slaps his hand to his forehead. "I know I shouldn't complain . . . But I really don't want to be Raoul. One of you should be him instead."

Kyle suddenly bursts into loud, sobbing tears. "I'm a failure," he chokes out. "I'm just not leading man material. How am I supposed to get into a good university if I'm not even good enough to get a leading role in high school? Andre? The opera house owner? He has no character development! He's just there to be business partners with Firmin!"

And then it's my turn. I see my name on the list beside Firmin.

"Why do I have to be a gross business guy?" I ask. "I just . . . I just wanted to be pretty." I feel something hot run down my cheek. I swipe it away with a finger and realize it's a tear. *Boys don't cry.* I can hear my mom's voice in my head scolding me.

I'm surprised when everyone nods. Drew speaks up. "Yeah, I just want to have fun with all of you and work through some feelings. I don't really like that I'm Piangi. He's not very nice and a little stuck up. I don't think I can hit his top note. He's a lead tenor. I'm barely a tenor!"

Jennifer speaks up, her voice still. "I can't help but notice that all the leads are white. Carlotta is being played by Crystal, who's white. Madame Giri is being played by Jillian, who's also white. Lefèvre, the former opera house owner, is being played by Debbie, who's brown. And Joseph Buquet the stagehand is being played by Monique, who's black. I'm Meg Giri, the best friend of Christine." She pauses. "And I'm really pissed off that there's no real gender play reflected in the casting. Despite what Ms. Brown said. I think she just wanted girls to volunteer to play smaller guy parts."

No one has anything to say.

Jennifer opens her arms to Kyle and me. The three of us stand there hugging. Finally, Kyle stops crying and says, "Ms. Brown's decisions were pretty bad. Even if I . . . I'm not good enough to be the Phantom or Raoul, I know Logan would make an amazing Christine. But maybe this is to prepare us. I'm beginning to fear how racist and bigoted the arts can be. Ms. Brown, she's a low-key, polite bigot. She's definitely integrated into Canadian culture."

I'm reminded of a scene from *Glee*. When Kurt fails to get the leading role, he says something about how there aren't any parts made for a guy like him. And that feels true to me right now. *Phantom* wasn't written about Asians. It wasn't written about queers. Why are we even doing this musical?

"I'm sorry, this must be even more shitty for you three," Robin says. "I'm filling Ms. Brown's office with gay pagan symbols in my head for you." He joins our group hug for a moment. And then Drew and Micah join in, too. With all of us together like this, I feel like things might be okay. We are a group of queers against the world. Maybe we're a little awkward and dysfunctional. But we can deal with this.

We can get through the winter concert and get through this musical together. Somehow. In a sense, this awful day brings us all closer together. And I say so to everyone, eliciting a few wet laughs.

"I need all the gay right now," Jennifer says to us. "Everything needs more gay."

Robin and Micah hold their joined hands up high and kiss each other dramatically.

Drew flicks their shoulders. "It's okay to be gay, just please not in my face," he says, sarcasm heavy in his voice. "You're oppressing my heterosexuality! Where's Straight Pride?"

Everyone cracks up and everything feels a little better.

17 Kind of There But Not Quite

A COUPLE WEEKS HAVE PASSED since we found out about the winter concert music and *Phantom*'s casting. It's been rough. My parents didn't take the casting very well. My dad patted me on the back and told me that there was always next time. Mom surprised me and threatened to come to school to yell at Ms. Brown. I almost agreed to let her do that.

It's finally the day that Jennifer and I are going shopping for clothes. So after choir practice, we hop on the subway as usual, but get off at Lansdowne Station. Jennifer is dressed down a bit more than usual. The November chill is setting in so she's wearing her leather jacket, a shirt, and leggings. Her hair is tied up in a single bun and she has minimal makeup. It's all to make it easier to change in and out of a lot of clothes, she tells me.

Value Village seems legit. According to my gaydar, there are definitely queer people browsing the racks. "Hey, since we're here," suggests Jennifer, pushing our cart. "You should try looking at clothes in the women's section, too. Emo kids do it all the time. Clothes are clothes after all. And it's fun to see everything on sale."

"Okay. You finding anything in your size here?"

"Yeah. This is why we're vintage shopping. There are a lot more clothes here for regular people. Did you know that the average woman is a size twelve? That's the biggest size they carry at most stores like H&M or Aberzombie."

"I never knew that," I reply. "They're missing out on a lot of money. Fashion designers are stupid."

"Well, they won't be getting any of my money. It's

their loss," Jennifer says with a sniff.

I feel self-conscious looking through the dress and skirt racks. But no one is paying attention to me. An older brown woman gives me a smile as she moves past. I add a few dresses, shirts, and pants that I like in a few different sizes to the clothes I'm going to try on. I'm not sure what size I am.

Shopping with Jennifer is chill. We chat and catch up. Between the two of us, we fill the entire cart with clothes. Then we go to the change rooms to begin the process of trying on everything.

We take turns in the change room, and come out to model our finds. I notice that Jennifer keeps only about one in five outfits. When I point this out, she says dryly, "Women's clothes aren't consistently sized. It's as if they're afraid that we take up more space than a twig."

It takes a bit for me to find what sizes work for me, but I figure it out somewhat. Even in clothes marked as being for men, I'm wearing about four sizes smaller than what my mom likes to buy me.

I step out of the change room wearing a dress. I'm

sure Jennifer catches my sour expression in the mirror. "I don't know about this," I say. "I don't think I look good in a dress."

"That's okay. You don't need to wear a dress. I like them, but maybe they're not for you. Or maybe not for you right now. But hey, it's fun to try out new things, right?"

"Yeah. I never knew how many different kinds of clothes there are."

"You'll learn as you go along," Jennifer encourages me. "No pressure to be an expert right away. Hell, my fashion sense is still always changing."

In the end, I pick out a couple of pairs of black skinny jeans from the women's rack and a fitted Batman T-shirt I also found in that section. We try on shoes, but I find that heels are definitely not for me. In another round of going through the racks, I find a three-piece black suit that's a lot more form-fitting than the one my mom made me wear. So everything I find comes from the women's racks. It surprises me. I really do prefer women's clothes. What does this mean for me?

My mom definitely isn't going to be happy about the new clothes. I have all these outfits that are still perfectly good that I never wear. And here I am buying used, form-fitting clothes. But I actually like how it looks. I feel like I am finally able to see myself a little better in the mirror now. I discover I like the look of my hips and butt.

We pay for our clothes. Jennifer has found a single dress. She says it's fine that she isn't buying a lot. It's a success if she finds anything that both fits and she likes. And she says she wanted to support me finding my own style first and foremost.

Jennifer asks if I want to try makeup. I shake my head. That would be a bit too much right now. I'm not really into dresses or really girly things. I like to think my look is somewhere between nerd chic, emo, punk, and goth. Almost everything I buy is black. I think I look pretty androgynous. And that feels right for me right now. I don't feel comfortable doing anything more than that. Jennifer seems a little disappointed that I don't want to try makeup. But she accepts my choice.

I feel pretty excited and happy with the new clothes that I am buying myself with the allowance I've been saving up for a while. But I'm still a little anxious about how my parents will react. I'm afraid they'll see that these new clothes all came from the women's section. I'm finally becoming the real me and I'm terrified. But also really excited. I don't feel like I'm a girl, even though I'm pretty sure Robin and Jennifer think that. But I'm definitely okay with wearing women's shirts and pants.

When I arrive home, Wendy scowls at me and asks why I'm smiling like that. She makes some rude comment that I ignore as I go to my room in the attic to put my new clothes away.

I sigh to myself. I'm pretty sure I have the dopiest smile on my face and I'm glad no one can see it. Then I realize I'm wondering if Kyle would think I look cute in my new clothes and catch myself. I can't have feelings for Kyle. He's taken. It's not okay. Conceal. Don't feel. Don't let it show. But I can't *let it go*.

18 Change My Luck

I HAVE TO HAUL my clothes back downstairs to show my parents what I bought. Their excitement at my interest in clothes quickly turns to disappointment. Dad frowns when he sees a pair of skinny jeans I bought. Mom says, "These clothes. They look too small. You silly boy. Can't even buy his own clothes in the right size. And why did you buy a new suit? The one I bought you is very nice!"

I didn't expect them to love my taste in clothes.

But I was hoping they wouldn't be so against it. I take a deep breath, remembering what Jennifer and I talked over earlier. "I'm trying to make my own decisions now," I tell them. "They may not be the decisions you would make. But could you let me learn from my own mistakes? As decisions go, buying clothes is pretty minor."

There is dead silence for a moment. Then Mom finally nods once. I feel something relax in me. The plan worked. Mom wants me to be more responsible and I guess I pass.

Voice class and choir have been a little awkward since the fight. Fewer girls come to talk and hang out with Micah than usual. But on the plus side, Ms. Brown lets Jennifer defect to the tenors without a fuss. I notice Ms. Brown has been a little less sunny and doesn't spend as much time with us anymore.

Drusilla comes to the tenor section to talk to us. It's

the second time I've seen her speak during choir and I am surprised by how deep and gentle her voice sounds. "Be careful with Ms. Brown," she warns. "I know she's . . . less than understanding. But you have your careers ahead of you. If you push her too much, she could get you suspended. I'm not saying you shouldn't call her out. But find ways so that she can't accuse you of doing anything wrong without looking bad. I know you can do it. Drew's told me about all of you. I believe that with all your creativity, you'll find a way to get through choir and the musical. And you'll all be much stronger for it."

And as quickly as she appeared, she leaves without waiting for an answer. She is mysterious like Drew, but I suspect for totally different reasons.

My crush on Kyle has not gone away. In fact, I feel like it's getting worse. Walking past the gym, I see him practising boxing shirtless. I have to run away to avoid staring at him and getting caught.

And, like the glutton for suffering I am, I sometimes spend time with Kyle. Alone. We are hanging out at Glad Day Bookstore, looking at queer comics when he asks me, "Is it weird that I'm straight? I mean, I don't like hanging around straight guys, especially jocks. All that toxic masculinity."

I am taken aback by the question. It's confirmation that he will never be into me. "Uh . . . No? You have two dads. You've probably had to deal with homophobes because of your dads, right?"

He nods. "Yeah. That's the reason why I don't do organized sports. My dads wanted me to get into sports. They read somewhere that it helps to prevent seizures. But I couldn't deal with being on a team. I learned how to box when I was twelve, after I had my last seizure. Before that, bullies kept picking on me. With new meds that finally worked and knowing how to fight, I haven't been bullied much since. Rosedale has been the first place I've felt safe."

"You know you're really strong, right?" I say to him. "Not just like physically. But like, you're alive and been through all that. You didn't become a bully. You found a good way to fight back without fighting back.

You're amazing y'know?" Sometimes, I surprise myself with how adult I sound.

He gives me a look that I can't quite decipher. "Yeah . . . Thanks. You're kinda quiet, but Jennifer is right. You give good advice. You notice things others don't."

After that, I know that I am gone for Kyle. He's so much more than just a really, really hot guy. I really admire how he keeps everyone in line in choir and looks out for all of us. No wonder Robin keeps calling him Daddy. So I have to try to not be alone with him.

Jennifer takes it upon herself (likely with Robin's plotting — I spot them giving each other looks sometimes) to help me find my image. So she offers to take me to get my hair cut by the Afro-Indian Guyanese queer hairdresser who does her hair. I've been letting my hair grow out since school started. My mom has been nagging me and my dad gives me disapproving looks for how long my hair is. Now I'm finally getting it cut.

"I don't know what I want," I confess to Gideon as I sit in his chair. "Maybe something more emo? I . . . I want to look more feminine. Or genderqueer. I don't know what it is exactly. But like, not something masc?" Gideon is a tall, stocky man and I am drawn to the way he moves. He sashays and has an easy grace that I wish I had. And being a hairdresser, his hair is so amazing. He has bright pink dreads that he keeps tied in a loose bun for work.

He walks around the chair, looking at my hair with an easy smile. "Your hair is pretty fine. You could pull off an asymmetrical emo cut, if you like. You could get it undercut, too. Maybe get some layers in?"

I pull up a picture on my phone of a Chinese emo girl with an asymmetrical bob. I show it to Gideon. "Does that work?"

He nods and gets to work. When he's done, Jennifer squeals. "Gideon works his magic again. Logan, you look so cute!"

I stare at myself in the mirror. I'm in shock. I look . . . pretty. No longer the weird, mousy kid. Now, with skinny jeans and my usual superhero T-shirt, I look like I belong at Hot Topic. I smile and thank Gideon for the amazing job.

I feel like a new person. I don't have a name for who I am becoming. But I like what I feel like. The first day at school with the new haircut, I go to hang out with Kyle and talk about the latest episode of *Agents of S.H.I.E.L.D.* But the moment he sees me, his eyes widen. His cheeks turn pink and he takes a step back from me. He stutters as we talk and won't look me in the eyes. But from that moment, it feels like he is pulling away from me and I don't know why. Well, it's for the best. I can't get any closer to him with this crush.

19 Feeling Deep Inside

THE DAY OF THE WINTER CONCERT arrives and we have a little plan going. Like last concert, Robin paints everyone's nails. This time, all six of us have glittery white nails. Then we change into our dress clothes right there in the voice classroom — all the tenors including Jennifer. She has elected to wear a black suit like we are all wearing, instead of the white, red, green, or gold dresses the other girls are wearing. We decided to wear black as a tiny defiance to Ms. Brown's Christmas cheer.

Once we are fully changed, Robin whistles. I turn to face him and he is looking at me with a soft smile. "Hey, Logan, you look pretty in that suit. Much better than that thing your mom forced you to wear."

I look away and flush. No one has ever complimented my appearance like that before. "Th-thanks. I like the rainbow Star of David you and Micah are wearing."

He grins wickedly. "It's another little way to defy Ms. Brown."

The room has a few floor-length mirrors and I look myself over. The suit hugs my frame and I can't help but stare at my butt. My mom clucked her tongue whenever I used to put on pants that showed that I had a butt. I like actually seeing I have one. It's small and round, and seeing it hugged by my pitch black pants makes me happy. It's mine and I'm not ashamed to show it.

I meet Kyle's inky eyes in the mirror. I don't say anything. What is he even doing?

Ms. Brown enters the room with her soprano angels and altos following behind her after grabbing dinner somewhere. And that's our cue to get into position for a last run through of the songs (ugh). Ms. Brown gives us a collective look but doesn't say anything. We stick to the plan, smiling politely as if nothing is wrong. She can't say anything. We are wearing formal performance clothes and she can't deny Robin or Micah their Star of David without looking anti-Semitic.

We do our job and perform. There's a lot of eye rolling and sour faces when no one is looking. Drew has reluctantly accepted a solo along with one of the sopranos for "Baby, It's Cold Outside." Robin remarks quietly how he'd rather risk the cold and get hypothermia than stay in the same room as the misogynist in the song. And why does the solo require a male and female singer in the first place?

After it's all over, we try to exit quietly. But my parents come to speak to us. Crap.

"Good show," booms my dad. "You've got a good teacher there. Logan, my boy, you should consider becoming a teacher like her. Good benefits to support your own family."

I repress a cringe. I don't have to look to see that my friends are doing the same thing. Except Robin. He doesn't care unless he has a reason to.

"I've thought about it," I say, trying to keep my voice neutral. "You know I want to try to become a professional singer and performer."

"Sure, that's what you think right now." Dad gives me his patented disapproving look. "You're going to regret that decision someday. It's okay if you do the namby pamby fruity art thing right now. But you're going to need to settle down someday. And for that, you'll need a steady income."

I try to think of a way to get out of there when my mom interjects. "What is that you're wearing on your nails? Nail polish is for girls, you silly boy."

Kyle is the one who speaks up. "It's my fault, ma'am. My girlfriend insisted I had to do my nails. As one of my best friends, Logan had their nails done in solidarity so I wouldn't be left out. So everyone else had their nails done, too."

He wraps an arm around my shoulder. I feel like

I'm going to die. He smells so good!

Then Kyle turns to my dad. "And with all due respect, sir, Logan works really hard at singing. They have a real shot at being amazing."

My mom looks Kyle over and says, "So you're the Japanese friend. Huh." She mutters something in Chinese I can't understand, but I catch something about *lǎolao* and *lǎoye*, my mom's parents who still live in China. Then she says, "You're right. Logan has some talent. I just hope he'll be more like you. The way he dresses is very . . . *niáng niang qing.* He should dress more like you."

I looked that word up last week. Mom has been calling me *niáng niang qing* for months. She has been calling me a sissy and didn't want me to know it.

"That's enough of that," my dad announces. "Let these boys get changed. And I expect that you'll clean your nails before you come home?" He gives me a hard look.

I nod. "Of course. We were just about to do that."

Kyle and I excuse ourselves from my parents.

Jennifer, Drew, Robin, and Micah are waiting for us in an empty row of seats.

"You okay?" Jennifer asks first.

I nod. "The usual. This is why I never introduced you to them. And all the rules. I can't wait until I can move out." I motion for us to leave the auditorium.

Ms. Brown is congratulating everyone and schmoozing with parents. We take over the seated section of the voice classroom. The sopranos and altos pull up the sectional wall and lock it in place so they can change in the main room.

"After this, we'll be on winter holiday. You sure you'll be okay?" Kyle asks me.

I am surprised that Kyle is the one checking in on me. It's been days since he has talked to me directly. "Yeah. I'm pretty skilled at avoiding the fam when I need to. Besides, I have all of you just a message away. We could also hang out at some point."

"I'd like that." He smiles.

I'm so screwed.

The holidays aren't fun for me. It means visiting friends of my parents and having to look presentable to them. And that means that I have to wear "the nice clothes" my mom buys me.

I said I was going to hang out with my friends, but it doesn't happen. My family ends up visiting Grandpa and Grandma (my dad's parents) and each of his three sisters' families. And we stay over at all of their places. I am reminded by my mom repeatedly during the visits that I am the only one carrying on the Osborne name. I get told repeatedly I have an obligation to ensure the name will be continued.

It's creepy to think about. But I make myself do it. Like, unless I end up with a trans guy, there is no way I'm having biological kids. And I'm not willing to have kids the old-fashioned way, *even* if this theoretical trans guy was willing. It's triggering to think about it.

When I do think about it, I realize I am definitely not a guy. I don't feel comfortable being a guy or being included as one. I don't like when people call me a guy and don't want to dress or present at all like a guy. I just don't know what kind of not-guy I am. Maybe I'm genderqueer or non-binary? I have been going to Alphabet Soup, but I haven't met any non-binary or genderqueer people who weren't assigned female at birth. Could I be non-binary? Or was that only for them?

And if I did transition to female, would I be straight? I've spent the past few months considering myself gay. I don't want to be a straight girl. I don't want to be like the girls in the performance stream. I don't want to be basic. I'm scared that I won't be included as part of the queer community anymore if I only like guys. What does it say about me that I'm still crushing on Kyle, who's straight? A disaster waiting to happen, that's what it makes me. Are these feelings about being more feminine so that maybe Kyle might notice me and break up with his girlfriend? In what fan fiction would I have to live for that to be even remotely possible? I'm such a fake.

So the holidays pass by with a lot of texting and apologies to my friends.

I'm glad to be heading back to school. Although I haven't missed Ms. Brown at all.

With the new term comes new projects. Namely, musical theatre.

20 Can't Contain This

WITH THE NEW YEAR, I begin experimenting more seriously with this new me. This kinda genderqueer/ non-binary me. Robin lets me borrow his old clothes. He brings them to school and I try and wear them all day to see how they feel. I'm lucky that we're the same size. In the end, I decide that his style isn't for me. He likes bright colours and mermaid and/or galaxy themed outfits. It's a little over-the-top for me. I'm already in hot enough water with the parents over the clothes I bought at Value Village. If I were to bring home some of Robin's clothes . . . yeah, no. I'm not planning on coming out to them. At least until I'm safely moved out and in university. Maybe not even then.

A few weeks into the winter term, I am busy planning out how to play Firmin to Kyle's Andre. They're the two new owners of the opera that *Phantom* takes place in. There isn't that much to their characters. In the movie version, they seem pretty stuffy and boring. Kyle and I are sitting on the stage when Ms. Brown interrupts us.

"That's inappropriate," she says in a soft voice.

I blink in confusion and look up at her with a frown. "What's inappropriate?"

"Those pants you're wearing. And that top. You're not supposed to show off any midriff. And the front of the pants is much too tight. I can see your underwear. I kindly ask you to change," she says, not at all kindly.

I start to apologize and get up to grab a change of clothes from my locker. But then Kyle responds.

"Logan's midriff isn't showing. Their shirt rode up a little. See?" He pulls down my shirt, showing that it actually covers up all my skin.

Ms. Brown really scowls at us. She's fidgeting furiously with the golden cross at her throat. She looks like she is trying hold in a nasty retort. The moment of awkward silence is broken when she says, "Fine." She walks off to talk to the mom of one of the girls who volunteered to help out with costumes and props.

"Logan, I'm sorry that I used they/them pronouns with you," Kyle says suddenly. "I did it after the winter concert, too."

Once again, I blink, confused by what is being said to me. I have to ask him to repeat himself before it sinks in. *They*. Kyle used *they* to refer to me, today and when talking to my parents about the nail polish. I didn't realize that Kyle did that and am not sure how I feel about it. And then I am sure. It sounds all right.

"It's fine," I say. "I guess you can keep on using they/them pronouns with me. I don't have anything better to use at the moment. Thanks for looking out for me just now and for checking yourself."

I have a lot to think about. Kyle is so hot and cold with me. He is really protective of me, but so are my other friends. And then he'll switch to being distant and not talking to me.

Phantom rehearsals eat up our time together as a group. Robin and Micah, as the male leads, spend a lot of time away from the rest of us. On the one hand, I am envious of their lead roles. On the other hand, I love that I don't have to spend time with Ms. Brown or pretend that I'm interested in Stephanie.

I try not to be petty. But Stephanie has everything I wish I had. She has the role I wanted. She is dating the guy I have a crush on. And she is blonde and straight and pretty and has everything given to her on a silver platter. One day, during rehearsal, she tells me she loves my new look. She asks me if I want to come to her slumber party. And I feel even more guilty because it's not just an act. She actually is a Disney princess. And what does that make me?

As I work on Firmin's character, I think about how I could make him more queer and interesting. Maybe he's in a relationship with Andre? But that would mean that I'd have to get closer to Kyle. And that is definitely off limits. Kyle likes girls and I . . . am not a girl. And even if I became a trans girl, I am nothing like Stephanie.

So I make Firmin an eccentric gay man with an unrequited crush on his business partner Andre. Firmin will be into wearing a lot of furs and jewelry. He'll be really pretentious. He'll act wealthier than he actually is because he came from the slums and faked and swindled his way up. He ends up becoming a co-owner of an opera house with his partner in crime. (Almost literally!)

I share this with Kyle. He gets excited and says, "That's really creative! And it also makes sense. They live in the late 1800s when everything is sexually repressed, especially being into men. And coming from the slums gives him a good reason to be stuck up. And since you came up with that idea, I think I should also make Andre gay. He'd have a secret crush on Firmin. They met while both selling fake jewelry on opposite corners of the street. Then teamed up and made a killing. What do you think?"

I grin at Kyle. I feel really warm and gooey inside that he takes my idea and makes it even better. "Yeah . . . I really like it. Like, really like it."

He grins back. It feels so wrong and so right at the same time. It feels like we have something between us. But he's straight and I'm not. And it never ends well when the gay boy (or non-binary person) falls for the straight boy.

Drew approaches me when everyone leaves after class. "Hey, Logan, I was thinking you might want to talk to Drusilla."

Now that's odd. "Why would I want to talk to your mom? Isn't she like, busy working?"

"Yeah, she is. But she does have time off. I just think you'd really benefit having an adult to talk to." He says it with an easy smile. I know he's leaving something out. But I trust that it isn't anything that will hurt me.

"All right. Thanks for thinking of me. I appreciate everything you've done to help me out. And if there's anything you need my help with, I'll be there."

"Are you free today?" he asks. "Drusilla will be home in a couple hours. I do all the cooking so you're welcome to stay for dinner."

"Sure. Um, maybe we can make something together? But I'm only beginning to learn to cook." I offer hesitantly.

Drew's face lights up in a way I've never seen before. "Really? You want to help me cook something? I'd love to show you how."

"I just hope I don't burn water or something equally embarrassing. See you at the front door in ten minutes?" I gather my books.

"Sure. See you in ten," he says as we walk out of the auditorium and off on our separate ways to our lockers.

21 Lipstick's Not Enough

DRUSILLA AND DREW LIVE in a nice townhouse near Broadview Station. Drew shows me around the house. He has already messaged Drusilla to let her know they are having me over. He offers me tea.

"How've you been?" I ask. "We don't get to talk much in class anymore now that we're working on the musical."

"Not bad. I'm reaching for Piangi's top notes. Ms. Brown is showing me how to hit them by fixing my posture and how I sing. It's actually really neat."

I blink. After the winter concert, I forgot that Ms. Brown is an amazing voice teacher — even if she's bigoted.

"Hey, Drusilla will be home in about an hour," Drew says. "Do you want to help me do a stir fry? It's something easy."

Drew is a patient teacher. He explains everything he is doing and why he is doing it. He washes and puts the rice in a rice cooker. I help him cut up vegetables while he does the chicken. The vegetables aren't cut that neatly, but he smiles and compliments me anyway. I think for a moment that he'll make a great teacher or dad someday.

The scent of meat and vegetables and sauces fills the room. Drew dances around the kitchen, grabbing bottles from a shelf of seasonings I vaguely recognize from grocery shopping on Spadina. The best I can do is stay out of the way and let Drew work his magic. I don't know how he got so good at cooking at our age, but it's amazing to watch.

It feels a little odd. Drew is white and I'm mixed

Chinese. But everything he does feels like what I've seen my mom do over the years in the kitchen. She puts my dad on prep because he doesn't know the difference between light and dark soy sauce. At least I'm already a better cook than my dad.

Drusilla shows up just as we are setting the table. "Hey, I'm home! Smells good in here."

Unlike the days she plays piano for us, she is dressed in a power suit. She seems to fill the whole room with her energy. But her eyes are crinkled as she smiles pleasantly at us.

The first thing Drusilla does is pull Drew into a big hug. They stay like that for longer than the typical hug. She turns to me and offers me her hand to shake. "Nice to meet you again, Logan."

I take her hand and shake it. "Nice to meet you again."

Drew clears his throat. "Logan, there's a reason why I want you to meet Drusilla. She might have some insight on what you're going through."

I look at Drusilla, trying to figure it out. Well, she's Middle Eastern and probably queer . . .

Finally, Drusilla fills me in. "What Drew is alluding to is that I'm a trans woman. From what he's told me, you're figuring out your gender right now. You're friends with a trans boy, Robin. But you've never met someone who's been through what you have. What it means to grow up with people treating you like a boy while also being a person of colour."

I'm in shock. That Drusilla could be a trans woman and look this badass. That she can deal with her gender and colour being what they are. I don't want to be like the other trans women I've seen. But Drusilla isn't like them either.

I have a million questions for her. "Is it normal for you to feel confused and weird about not being gay anymore? What about the stereotype that Asians are submissive and they feed into it by transitioning? Do I need to —"

Drusilla raises her hand to cut me off. "While I'd love to answer all your questions, the meal that you helped prepare is getting cold. Think we can talk over dinner and not leave Drew out of the conversation?"

I look over at Drew. He has the same amused look on his face as when we hung out at Alphabet Soup the first time. I look away, embarrassed at forgetting him in my excitement.

Over dinner, I ask Drusilla a bunch of questions that she answers as honestly as she can. She tells me off a few times for being too energetic. I get the impression she's thinking *children* while rolling her eyes at me.

Turns out she's Afghani. When she was found crossdressing, her marriage fell apart and she got fired from her job as a music teacher in Alberta. So she transitioned while going to law school. Her studies focused on human rights for trans and queer people, because she didn't want what happened to her to happen to anyone else. She was a part of the group pushing for Bill C-16 in the *Charter*, the one that makes trans people a protected grounds for human rights.

"You don't need to be like me," Drusilla says. "I'm a little old-fashioned. I'm from a different generation and culture from you. I'm fine being a frumpy lady when I'm not in a suit. But you, you're something different. I'm excited to see who you'll become."

She asks me questions. Like if I want to come out to the family. *Nope.* And if I want to have people treat me like they treat girls. *Maybe?*

The whole meal, Drew stays pretty quiet. But he doesn't look unhappy about being the quiet one. In fact, he keeps giving me knowing looks and clears away the dishes while Drusilla and I are still talking. He serves Drusilla lemongrass tea and offers me the same. He's so good at being a good host that I wonder where he learned it. I know Drew doesn't like to talk much about his past before coming to Toronto. But whenever he doesn't think anyone is watching, he often looks so sad. Or his blue eyes reflect some old hurt that makes him look older than he actually is.

The visit is really great and gets me excited. I thank both of them for all their help and offer to help them with anything they need in the future, as long as it's something I can do. Meeting Drusilla gives me a lot to think about and so I go home with a head full of thoughts.

22 *Girl Almighty*

AFTER THE *PHANTOM* REHEARSAL, I ask Kyle to gather everyone so I can make an announcement. I'm breaking news I'm pretty sure everyone already knows but it just needs confirmation.

"Thanks for being able to all meet together like this," I start. "I know that it's hard for us to hang out together with the musical going on. I just wanted to say that I would like you to use they/them pronouns with me. I don't know if I want to change my name yet. Thanks for being patient as I figure out if I'm genderqueer, non-binary, or what." I pace around in front of them as I speak. I manage to glance at each of their faces and find nothing but support. Even though I know they are good, it's still pretty scary to admit out loud that I'm not a boy.

I see Micah hand Robin five dollars. I narrow my eyes and frown at them. "Hey! You bet on me?!"

Robin smiles, pretending innocence. But I know better. "Just when you'd tell us," he says. "I bet this week. Micah bet next month."

I sigh and look at everyone else. "Did anyone else bet on when I'd come out as not-cis?"

Everyone else shakes their heads. At least there's that.

Jennifer speaks up. "Can I get you to try out makeup now? I really want to show you the wonders of eyeliner and mascara. I can make your pretty eyes really pop."

I feel my face get warm and think about her offer. "Um. Soon? I don't think I'm ready for that yet. And that's all I wanted to say. So you can leave and go home now."

Kyle gives me a thumbs up. Jennifer gives me a hug. And Robin and Micah kiss each of my cheeks. But Drew looks proud. I thank him for being so much help in figuring it all out.

Weeks pass and winter begins melting away. The musical is shaping up. Those of us who have smaller parts are pretty well off-book.

My Firmin costume consists of a lot of ruffles and embroidery and I make facial hair that I learn to apply to my face with spirit gum. Playing Firmin feels more and more like I am in drag. In fact, I learn how to be a drag king at a workshop at Alphabet Soup. I've gone back a few times, sometimes with Jennifer or Drew, sometimes without. I watch the girl playing Joseph Buquet, the stagehand. I notice how she just looks and acts like a girl wearing boy's clothes. And she uses ace bandages to try to bind. It doesn't work but she refuses when Robin offers to lend her one of his binders. It's as if she doesn't really want to pass as male. And for me, I don't like it. But I'm learning to treat being a man as a performance, which it is. Literally.

I talk with everyone, especially Robin, Drew, and Jennifer, about gender feelings. Robin asks me, "When you imagine being with a guy, do you want him to call you pretty? How do you want him to treat you?"

I think about Kyle. I imagine his arm around my hips. I think about him looking at me and calling me pretty. And my heart aches thinking about it. But I'm not into wearing dresses like Jennifer, or suits like Drusilla. I'm a nerd. I dream more about sharing a couch with Kyle reading comics, books, or fan fiction. Or sketching him while he works out. I'm not that into dressing fancy.

Jennifer gave me a black leather jacket similar to hers for my birthday in January. But I only start wearing it after the snow melts. The first day I put it on, I pair it with black skinny jeans and my fitted *Agents of S.H.I.E.L.D.* shirt. And when I look in the mirror, I see Chloe Bennet looking back at me. Well, not really. But I look a lot like her. We are both mixed Chinese and white. My hair is shorter than hers, but we both have big dark eyes. I look kinda like her. Looking in the mirror, it feels right. I look like Chloe Bennet and I feel right in my skin.

This is me.

This is me . . .

THIS IS ME!!

I am . . . I could be a girl? Maybe? Drusilla was right. I'm not a woman like her. I love the look of wearing a leather jacket like Jennifer does, but I'm also a nerd. I've tried and liked eyeliner and lashes, but I don't always like how lipstick feels on my lips. And I don't want to learn how to contour or do whatever that stuff Jennifer does is called.

I could be a girl. One who prefers jeans and tees. Maybe with sparkly nails if I can get away with it. And that . . . that's okay.

I go to school looking like this. In Visual Art

class, I tell Jin-Seon. Ms. Adams-Kushin calls me her smol-goth, because of how little and cute I look. Even though I'm taller than she is. We laugh about it and Jin-Seon asks, "Now that you're figuring out you're a girl, have you picked a name yet?"

I tell her what I've been thinking. I've been a fan of the Veronica Lodge character from *Archie Comics* since I was little. And the *Riverdale* TV show made Veronica even better. Both Ms. Adams-Kushin and Jin-Seon refer to me as Veronica during class. It feels a little weird. But good.

I'm at Alphabet Soup a few days later, hanging out with Drew and Jennifer. I have makeup on, courtesy of a trip with Jennifer to Nyx Cosmetics. I travelled all the way to Sherbourne like this without becoming the newest statistic for the Trans Day of Remembrance. So yay progress.

When the group does check-ins, I gather my

nerves and introduce myself as Veronica. Aidan, the cute group facilitator, gives me a special smile and calls me Veronica. It feels . . . nice to hear it from him. And from my friends. It feels right.

At the end of the drop in, I excuse myself to the bathroom to remove my makeup (now properly, with actual remover!). I have to butch it up for the family. But the two bathrooms are occupied. I stand around the hallway waiting for a stall to free up. Like déjà vu, Kyle exits the bathroom. It's like a replay of that day all those months ago. He does a double take when he sees me. His eyes widen in surprise.

"Hey," I say, my voice cracking. "I just want to mention that I'm trying out the name Veronica."

He doesn't say anything for a moment. Then he takes a deep breath. "I'm happy for you, Veronica. Ah. I gotta go, though. My *otosan* needs me." He waves and almost runs away from me. He can't even look me in the eye! What the hell?!

All thoughts of changing fly out of my mind.

I find myself sitting between Jennifer and Drew. I

hold their hands as I tell them what happened.

Jennifer looks pretty angry. She squeezes my hand. "I can't believe he pulled that shit! That wasn't in . . . I mean, I'm going to be giving him a piece of my mind."

"You need anything?" Drew asks. "I could pop into the kitchen and whip up something super fast." He started cooking for the group a few weeks ago as part of the forty hours of volunteer work we all need in order to graduate.

"Thanks. I'm good." I give him a weak smile. "I'm okay. Really!"

He doesn't buy it. "After Jennifer chews out Kyle, we can confront him about what's up with him. That's not cool what he did. But there's got to be a reason why he ran away from you. And it's not your fault at all. It's all on him."

During the rest of the group, we plot what we are going to do next.

I know I want to do this on my own. I've asked so much from my friends. All of them. I want to show the world that I can solve my own problems. But I talk it out with Jennifer and Drew. Micah and Robin are in the know, but they are ridiculously busy with *Phantom*. I know they're rooting for me.

23 Silence and Sound

I CATCH KYLE JUST OUTSIDE school after practice. He looks really good. But I'm not just head over heels drooling over his body anymore. I see the man he is becoming. Someone who shoulders a lot of responsibility and cares for those he holds dear. I see the weird nerd that I can talk comics with. And I see the boy who ran away from me after I told him that I was changing my name.

I stop him as he walks away from the school. "Hey,

we really need to talk. Do you have time right now?"

He turns. For a moment, I think I see fear flash through his eyes. But he nods. "Yeah. You deserve an apology. And an explanation for my rudeness."

We walk to a nearby park and sit on a bench. We have some privacy to talk. But not so much privacy that he could axe murder me if he wanted.

"First," Kyle starts, "the reason I've been avoiding you, and that I ran away from you the other day has nothing to do with you being trans. I support you wholeheartedly, Veronica. And did you name yourself after the character from *Archie* or from that music video that was always playing a few years ago?" He is clearly trying to delay.

"The *Archie* character," I say, rolling my eyes at him. "One time. One time I admit to reading fan fiction about that popular boy band that I refuse to admit I like." I have to get him to just say it. My heart feels like it's going to explode from my chest. "If it's not about me being trans, what is it?"

Kyle takes a deep breath. He is fidgeting with the

hem of his shirt. He tries to say something but stops. He does this a few times and I start getting annoyed with him.

"Just spit it out and say it," I say. "You're one of my closest friends. I'm afraid of losing you from my life!" Uh. That came out a lot sappier than I wanted it to.

Kyle locks eyes with me. He looks vulnerable and scared. And I want to wrap him in a hug to make it all go away. But this is something he needs to do.

"I . . . I developed inappropriate feelings," he says. "Toward you. I couldn't stop them, but they happened."

What?! What does he mean by *inappropriate feelings*? Is it . . . ? How can this happen? This is the real world. Not a gay rom com. Not fan fiction. The trans girl doesn't get the sexy boy. The Asian boy doesn't get the other Asian boy without something breaking them apart. Like death. And I've yet to see an Asian trans girl end up anything but dead.

"I get that you don't return these feelings," Kyle goes on. "That is. The romantic feels. And, uh. Sexy feels? But as you started to transition, I couldn't help but notice you more. And I spent a long time questioning my sexuality. Like, I'm straight, but not narrow. When you told everyone that you were questioning your gender, I felt a sense of relief. It made sense that I had feelings for you. And then you started to transition. You went from a cute nerd boy to a sexy nerd girl. I didn't think you'd ever be into an Asian with a defective brain. I'm sorry." Kyle hangs his head. He looks defeated.

I am in shock. How . . . ? Why . . . ? Then I remember. Stephanie.

"You're with Stephanie . . ." I finally croak out. Now it's my turn to not be able to meet his eyes.

"Oh, I haven't dated her in months," I hear him say. "We actually broke up right after the winter concert. All she cared about was that I'm Japanese. Kept on calling me *senpai*. Or *Onii-chan*. I had to look those words up and I'm Japanese! I'm not an upperclassman to her and I'm not her big brother. That's just creepy."

Wait. What? He's been single all term? "She should date one of the guys from my Visual Art class," I hear myself say. "They deserve each other."

Suddenly, we're both laughing. We guffaw and giggle until the supercharged emotions deflate a little.

"So let me make this clear," I say. "You have romantic and sexual feelings for me. And you are single?" I try to keep some distance between us in case I'm wrong.

He nods. He can't seem to say anything. And he can't meet my eyes.

"You asshole!" I yell at him and smack his shoulder. "I've wanted to kiss you most of this year!" It just comes out of me. And it feels great to finally release all these emotions.

"Then . . . can I kiss you?" Kyle's voice is soft.

Without replying, I lean forward. I press my lips against his and my hand cards through the short hairs on the back of his neck. He's kissing back, pulling me closer into his lap.

And it's so hot. I feel like I'm burning up. Like a supernova. I feel more than hear our teeth clack against each other's. His hands are in my hair, too. I can taste his cologne or body wash or pheromones or whatever it is. I can't get enough of it. I end up in his lap, straddling his hips. And he lets me.

And then I remember. Public location. People could be watching. He must have the same idea because we both pull away. We are both blushing horribly.

"Um . . . yeah," I say. Articulate or what?

Kyle looks at me with such a soft look of wonder that I feel my heart catching. And it's everything I ever dreamed of. He's everything I ever dreamed of. He blows the guy from the dance out of the water. Out of my mind forever. I wipe tears from my eyes.

"So this is the part where Firmin and Andre get together as an actual couple," Kyle says.

I giggle. "Only you would be thinking about work at a time like this." I kiss his cheek. "And that's one of the things I've learned to accept about you. You wouldn't be you if you weren't responsible and helping to keep me in line."

Kyle gets off the bench and gets on one knee.

What in the world is he doing? "Veronica," he says. "Will you be the Billy to my Teddy, the Mystique to my Destiny? Will you go out with me? I've never met another girl like you. And I don't think I ever will. You're something special."

I pull him back up onto the bench. My emotions are all over the place but I manage to nod and start babbling. "Yeah. Totally. Completely. I can't believe this is happening. I'm dying. This is a dream. I've wanted you from, like, the moment we met. I think if I ever come out to my mom, she'll hate you for being Japanese and not because we won't ever give her grandbabies to carry on the family name."

Kyle giggles and wraps an arm around me. "Don't die on me. I can't tackle the zombie apocalypse without you. Or maybe we could both be zombies and take down all the wannabe zombie killers."

And then our phones both ping at the same time. As one, we check our phones to see a single text from Jennifer.

I put Kyle up to confessing his feelings. Now you can both stop mooning after each other. You're welcome. 8-)

We share a look. I could get lost in his dark eyes now that I can look and touch guilt-free. So I break our moment and say, "I heard Sophie Campbell is going to be at comic-con. Think we could get tickets? I'd love to see Jennifer's face when she finds out she can meet her favourite comic book artist."

"She'd love that," Kyle agrees. "We can make it a double date. Now, this is cheesy, but I've been wanting to do this . . ."

And then Kyle is singing the chorus to "What Makes You Beautiful."

That *one* time I mentioned that band! I'm never again telling him what fan fiction I read. My cheeks turn pink and I squeal. I hide my face but still watch him sing from between my fingers.

After he is done, I stand up. He pulls me into his arms and I fit perfectly there. And we are kissing once again. And again. And again.

Acknowledgements

This book wouldn't have been possible if not for a bunch of my friends and fam. Thanks to Cat, Hilda, Alexa, Vyi, Markus, Saoirse, and a bunch of other people I've chatted at about this book.

I'd also like to acknowledge that this book takes place on stolen Indigenous land of the Anishinaabe, Haudenosaunee, and Huron-Wendat people. This land is subject to the Dish With One Spoon Wampum Belt Covenant, which is an agreement between the Ojibwe, Iroquois Confederacy, and other allied nations to peacefully share and care for the land and resources around the Great Lakes. Tkaronto (the Haudenosaunee name for Toronto) is still the home to many Indigenous people from all over Turtle Island including the Métis and Inuit nations.

A number of locations are mentioned in the book. Although the characters and situations are fictional, these places are real. They may not be exactly like I have described in the book. I took some artistic liberties and any mistakes are of my own making. Here's the info if you wish to learn more about each of them:

Youth Line
www.youthline.ca
1-800-268-9688
647-694-4275

SOY
soytoronto.org
333 Sherbourne Street, 2nd Floor
Toronto, ON M5A 2S5
416-324-5077 (phone)
416-324-4262 (fax)
soy@sherbourne.on.ca

Justice For Children and Youth
jfcy.org/en/

55 University Ave, 15th Floor
Toronto, ON M5J 2H7
Telephone: 416-920-1633
Ontario Toll Free: 1-866-999-JFCY (5329)

Glad Day Bookstore
www.gladdaybookshop.com
499 Church St
Toronto, ON M4Y 2C6

Buddies in Bad Times Theatre
buddiesinbadtimes.com
12 Alexander St
Toronto, ON M4Y 1B4

31901066884349